A WIND FROM THE SEA

A Wind from the Sea

Jennifer Morgan

First impression—2003

ISBN 1 84323 209 X

This book is published with the financial support of the
Welsh Books Council.

Printed in Wales at
Gomer Press, Llandysul, Ceredigion SA44 4QL

Contents

1

A Sea Change

Nobody knew where the body came from. After a night of driving rain and an onshore wind it had appeared – quite literally – out of the blue. Now, encircled by driftwood and a collection of Mersey flotsam, it had come to rest against the stone steps of Britannia Wharf, a seagull perched, unconcernedly, on its head.

Dead bodies were common enough in Liverpool in 1833, when sailing ships brought leprosy and smallpox, as well as coffee and indigo, from around the world. But inside the dark quayside store of Duffy the chandler, who sold everything from bacon to buttons, this particular corpse provided an excuse for an hour's gossip.

As Duffy polished away at a tin lamp with his thin bony hands, his eyes darted around at the handful of customers who lounged amongst the sacks of flour and dried peas. But he failed to make out the small, listening figure of Patience Penry, who had slipped in to buy two pennorth of candles and who now hid in the shadows, enveloped in her mother's shawl and alert with curiosity.

Two things only were certain: the body was female, and it was black.

'Fer all we know,' wheezed a short man in a long knitted scarf, 'the sea could've turned 'er black!'

'The sea don't cut a number in yer shoulder – that's fer sure!' said a fat woman standing in the doorway and blocking the light.

'Wouldn't I know you'd be taking an interest in the case, Sal Bludgeon,' said Duffy. 'But a number on her shoulder you say? That's queer, seeing as it must be twenty years since the slavers plied this way.'

'I'm not talkin' about nuffin' legal!' declared Sal. 'But you an' me knows, Mr Duffy, that one 'alf of the black lads and lasses wot plies for work around the docks got 'ere by stowing thesselves away among the cotton bales from Americky, thinkin' they'm safe on English soil!' She settled herself creakingly on a high stool by the counter and Patience took a step forward to hear better.

'But,' Sal went on, 'a body'd need to be blind as a beggar not to see that they vanishes like that' – she snapped a fat finger – 'whenever a ship sets sail for the Noo World, but non of us notices, oh no! And why? 'Cos all of us stands to gain – there's rewards offered for them back where they come from! And we know oo gets the money and' – she leant towards Duffy, who recoiled under the impact of her breath – 'and where they spends the money when they returns to Liverpool!'

'Well now,' said Duffy lightly, 'isn't that all dockside gossip!' Sal shrugged and the ragged feather in her bonnet bobbed.

'Oi've often wondered,' mused the character in the scarf, ''ow they gets they poor critters to stop still long enough to brand 'em wiv numbers.'

'I can tell you 'ow they does it!' volunteered Sal, with gruesome relish, but Duffy held up a finger to silence her. He peered into the shadows.

'Patience Penry, come away out o' that or you'll never get served this day!' He glared with mock severity over his half-moon spectacles. There was no hope for it. Patience's slight figure moved reluctantly towards the counter. Fair, wispy hair surrounded her freckled face and her grey eyes opened wide as she met the shopkeeper's gaze. She looked considerably younger than her thirteen years.

'Half a pound of candles and a pennorth of salt, please,' she said.

The others watched in silence as Duffy weighed the items on wobbly tin scales.

'And Mother says please to take another tuppence against what she owes you,' Patience added. Duffy made a mark on the slate that hung discreetly behind a string of onions.

The door of the shop was in two halves. As Patience hurried out, Sal Bludgeon pulled the bottom half to and clanged the latch, but the top half remained ajar and, by descending a step, Patience was small enough to be out of sight from within. She wanted to learn more about the body. To her annoyance, Duffy and his customers changed the subject and began to discuss *her*.

'I tried to get our Lily to answer folk nice like that,' Sal wheezed, 'but "please" and "thank you" don't come natural to 'er some'ow.'

'Sure isn't Patience's ma edicated,' replied Duffy, 'and haven't they books.'

'Books!' exclaimed the knitted scarf. 'Books! – and her chalking up pennies on the slate!'

'But only since the cholera took her da,' Duffy explained. 'One of the best shipwrights in these parts, John Penry was. I mind the day he came in here some fifteen years back to ask directions to Grundy's yard and he with small English – I could scarce make out his Welsh accent.'

A dray horse and its clattering wagon rounded the corner, drowning all other sounds, and Patience decided to head for home.

A wooden walkway ran along the front of the quayside buildings and her boots clomped along the boards as she picked her way amongst driftwood, broken crates and the assorted debris that last night's storm had thrown up. High above she could hear the 'thwack thwack' of ships' rigging against the masts. The wind was still keen and she drew a corner of her mother's shawl across her nose. As she turned into Chapel Hill, which rose steeply before her, she slackened her pace. Duckboards gave way to cobbles and cobbles to paving stones. Home, for

Patience and her mother, was three rented rooms above a draper's shop in what Florence Penry termed a 'respectable' street. The smell of ironing greeted Patience as she pushed open the street door and climbed the stairs.

Florence Penry heard her daughter's approaching footsteps with relief. Since her husband's death two months ago, she'd been obliged to ask the tradesmen for credit and preferred to do so as far from her own locality as possible. John Penry's name, she knew, was good amongst the shopkeepers near to the shipyard where he'd worked, but she sent Patience into the area only rarely and with some trepidation. Dropping the iron onto its stand, she stretched her aching back and tucked a strand of hair inside her cotton house-cap. She was recognisably Patience's mother, and her small features, drawn and tense as they were, showed that she had been remarkably pretty. She smiled as Patience's face, pink from her climb, appeared around the door. Then she clapped a hand to her mouth and let out a squeal of mirth.

'Patience!' she cried, 'just *look* at my shawl!'

Patience glanced down at the fringe of the garment she had borrowed and saw that it was bordered with a wonderful collection of leaves, wood shavings, paper wrappers – even a pair of broken spectacles!

'The Queen of Sheba has arrived!' Florence exclaimed, whisking off the shawl and holding it up.

'Are you cross?' Patience asked, then saw that the shawl and her mother behind it were shaking with

11

laughter. Patience joined in until they were both obliged to sit down on the brass fender to recover.

Both knew that the joke had received more mirth than it deserved. Laughter had been rare in their home since John Penry's death and the shawl with its unusual decorations had provided a welcome release of tension.

Patience could still hardly believe that her father would not be coming back. But sometimes the reality struck home and the emptiness became overwhelming. Then she would retreat to whichever room was unoccupied and sob into the curtains or the bedspread. She knew that her mother wept as well, but her grief was overshadowed by a constant, nagging worry about their future and how they were going to manage. Money was very short, their savings growing smaller daily, and Patience dreaded adding to her mother's anxiety by showing her distress.

But for much of each day the loss seemed only half real, and Patience had to remind herself not to expect the heavy clump of boots on the stair at half past six, followed by the cheerful Welsh greeting, '*Sut mae pethau?*' – 'How are things?' as her father threw his heavy satchel of carpenter's tools behind the door. 'Things are all right,' had been Florence's regular reply, 'but I don't know where Patience can be!'

There followed a well-worn ritual: Patience would always be in the same place – squeezed into the twelve inches between the piano and the grandfather clock, but her father would make pretence of looking in the most unlikely places.

'Not here!' he would mutter. 'Not there!' drawing closer, until finally he would pounce on Patience with a roar. This, combined with his daughter's shrieks would cause Florence to warn, 'Sshh! – remember Mr Brinthorpe's nerves!' Mr Brinthorpe, the draper who dwelt below, was the Penrys' landlord. Too much noise would provoke Mrs Brinthorpe to bang on the ceiling with a broom handle. These days the broom remained silent, at least for that purpose.

Now, Patience glanced up to where freshly-ironed garments dangled cheerfully from the clothes rack above her head and her brows knit in puzzlement.

'Mother, why have you washed so many of my clothes – and my best dress as well?'

Florence stood up, her face suddenly serious again.

'I'm going to talk to you about that, dear,' she said, gesturing to Patience to follow her into the living-room. Immediately Patience's legs turned to water and she sat down heavily next to her mother on the velveteen sofa. In a faint voice, which quavered, despite her best efforts to keep it steady, she asked, 'Am I – are you – going to send me away?'

'Yes and no,' her mother replied, which helped the legs not at all, for now they were trembling visibly.

'What do you mean?' Patience squeaked, real alarm gripping her stomach. Florence put an arm around her.

'Not away,' she said gently, 'and not for good, but to Uncle Huw in Wales for a while until we can be together again. You see,' she went on, 'I've managed to obtain employment which will help to keep us.'

Patience's panic subsided a little. She sensed that her mother was finding it hard to break the news, and she made an effort to appear calm.

'But why does that mean I must live with Uncle Huw?'

'Because,' explained Florence, 'I shall be living in. I'm going to be an assistant housekeeper at Culver Park.'

The name evoked for Patience a distant Sunday walk when her father had taken her to the woods above the town to see the bluebells one May morning. He'd pointed with his walking stick through a gap in the trees towards a grey house set in parkland.

'Sir Joshua Makepeace lives there,' he'd told her. 'He's done a lot for this town – and for the poor black people.'

Patience had meant to ask her father what this meant, but at the time the only thing that seemed to matter in the world was to gather as many bluebells as her arms could hold. She realised that her mother was still speaking.

'. . . my bed and board,' Florence was saying, 'so that I shall be able to save my wages. When I've saved enough, I'm hoping to be able to set up as a dressmaker – Mr Brinthorpe can get me cloth at cost – so that we can live together again. So, you see, it's not that bad! And you'll be getting fresh, country air and learning to milk and make butter on the farm! Your aunt can't wait for you to go – she's always wanted a daughter of her own. And I might even be able to visit you in the autumn!' She smiled into Patience's face hopefully.

Patience was in a turmoil. Part of her wanted to fling her arms around her mother's neck and protest, but she knew that she must not. Florence had grown thin over the past weeks and clearly this was a way out of their difficulties. Patience smiled weakly and kissed her mother's cheek. The news had left her shocked and frightened, but at least her legs had stopped shaking. Florence squeezed her hand.

'You're a good girl!' she said, with relief. 'I knew you'd be grown-up about it!'

Patience had never felt less grown-up in her life. She looked around for Woolly Mary, her rag doll, then saw through the open kitchen door that she, too, was dangling from a peg on the drying rack.

'How will I get to the farm?' she asked, 'and when must I go?'

Florence stood up.

'Mr Morris, the minister, is going to Ruthin next week to begin a three-month preaching tour. He'll take you with him on the coach, half fare, and Uncle Huw will meet you at Ruthin and take you on from there. Mr Morris will be calling by tomorrow for the money so he can book your seat. We've a lot to do in the next few days!'

Next week! Patience's face was fixed on her mother's. Florence bent and took her daughter's hands in hers.

'I know this has been a shock, dear, but we must both realise how lucky we are. God has answered our prayers and has looked after us. If He hadn't, it could well have meant the workhouse in six months' time!'

'The workhouse!' Patience looked at her mother in utter disbelief. 'But that's where people go . . .'

'Off the streets,' Florence nodded. 'And we could well have been amongst them – yes, really, Patience! So remember to say "thank you" when you next say your prayers.' She turned and went into the kitchen.

Patience sat very still, taking in her mother's words. She had mixed feelings about God. It was all very well to talk of thanking Him for providing her mother with work, but if He hadn't taken Father away, He wouldn't have needed to. The words of a familiar hymn ran through her head:

'God moves in a mysterious way
His wonders to perform;
He plants his footsteps on the sea
And rides upon the storm.'

She lay back on the sofa. Patience's world was a small one. She had only known the three rooms of her home, chapel on Sundays and, for a brief period, Mrs Dobson's Day School. When it was discovered that Mrs Dobson was in the habit of shutting recalcitrant pupils in the broom cupboard, Patience had been removed. From that time on, Florence had taught Patience herself – with frequent reference to Bright's *Popular Home Educator*, and *The Book of Saints and Heroes*. These volumes, with the Bible, *The Pilgrim's Progress*, *The Works of William Shakespeare* and a slim volume entitled *How to Dress Like a Lady on £10 a Year* by Mrs Buckforth, had pride of place at the back of the sideboard, supported by a bust of Nelson on one side and Florence's overflowing sewing box on the other.

Patience surveyed the familiar objects that had spelt 'home' for the whole of her thirteen years. They seemed suddenly to have taken on a new impermanence. Lord Nelson, who sometimes doubled as a hat stand, stared distantly at the opposite wall, and the Infant Samuel, who had gazed down from his mahogany frame on so many birthdays and Christmases, seemed to have his mind on other matters. Perhaps he, too, thought it was not that bad.

Patience tried to remember all that she had been told about her uncle, her aunt and the farm. Uncle Huw was her father's elder brother and she loved hearing tales of their boyhood at Hafod. Father had explained that the name meant 'summer home' and had recounted tales of lambing and shearing, or harvest suppers and *noson lawen*, when neighbouring farmers and their families would gather to sing, recite and drink *cwrw* until the moon rose. Hints would be dropped of a holiday there, and Patience had imagined the three of them setting off together for this distant, enchanted place. Now she would be making the journey alone. She was going to have to grow up rather more quickly than she had expected.

2

A Name Beginning with 'X'

A captive fly buzzed against the window pane and Patience sat up. She went into the kitchen, where her mother was peeling potatoes.

'May I go for a walk before dinner?' she asked.

Florence read her daughter's thoughts. She wiped her hands on her apron and took two sprays of lilac from a jam jar on the windowsill, shaking the water from the stems.

'These can go on the grave,' she said. 'Throw the dead ones away, would you dear? And be back by two o'clock!'

Puffball clouds scudded above the red brick terrace of Jamaica Street as Patience walked out into the sunshine. Father would have liked to think of her going to stay at Hafod. She sniffed at the fragrant blooms as she made her way towards the square shape of Zion Chapel. Unlatching the iron gate, she took a path that led behind the chapel to where headstones stood in neat rows and a mighty yew tree towered above them.

Here it was silent and still and a dapple of sunlight flickered across the flagged path. Patience felt closer to her father when she came here. His immediate neighbours were 'John Tay, Boatswain of the *Dora*' and 'Martha Jane, Beloved Wife'. Martha and John had carved headstones, but Father was still waiting for his. Each week Patience's mother put five shillings in a tobacco tin for the stonemason and each week took them out again to pay the butcher or to top up the rent. Meanwhile, a copper vase of faded flowers sat on a neat mound of earth. Patience bent to remove the dead blooms – and froze like a statue. Embedded in the soil of her father's grave was the fresh imprint of a naked foot.

She stared, motionless. She judged the foot that made it to be a little larger than her own and found that she could just place her boot inside the outline. Few people went barefoot in this part of Liverpool and poor folk from the dockside seldom ventured this far up the hill. She could think of no explanation.

As the shock subsided she set about smoothing the earth and replacing the flowers, then sat down on an adjacent, flat-topped gravestone to think. She wanted to get used to the idea of going away. Half of her felt excited and half of her, frightened. Just now she wasn't sure which half was winning.

Specks of dust danced up and down in the sunbeams that pierced the shade of the yew tree. As she gazed at its massive girth, Patience's attention was suddenly riveted. The smooth silhouette of the tree's trunk was interrupted by an unfamiliar hump at its base. The more she stared at the dark shape, the more she was convinced that it was not part of the tree and that it had not been there before. Then, almost imperceptibly, it moved.

Patience gripped the edge of the stone slab and swallowed hard. The shape narrowed and lengthened as the figure under the tree stood up and began to move very slowly towards her. Her heart was pumping now and she was on the point of screaming when she saw, through the sunbeams, that the approaching figure was that of a young girl.

'What do you want?' she called nervously.

'Please,' said the figure falteringly, 'please . . .' – and collapsed in a heap on the stone path.

Patience was beside her in an instant. Her fear was forgotten as she tried all she could to revive the still form. The girl was icy cold and apparently unconscious. She was brown-skinned, her feet were bare and her grey, cotton dress was sodden. As Patience vigorously massaged the chill, damp limbs, the girl's eyes half opened and she moaned weakly.

'Don't try to get up!' Patience ordered. 'I'll be back very soon!'

She raced out of the graveyard, calling to her mother as soon as she drew level with the Brinthorpes' shop. Florence flung open the window. She caught the gist of Patience's gasped message and within minutes the two were hurrying towards the chapel, Florence, still in her apron, clutching a blanket.

The girl was half sitting up, holding her head and

shivering violently. Florence quickly wrapped the blanket around her shoulders and helped her to her feet. But it was clear that her legs would not support her and she sank to the ground.

'What can we do?' Patience wailed. 'Shall I fetch Mr Brinthorpe?'

'No,' replied her mother. 'He'll make matters worse. Lay the blanket on the ground, Patience, and help me lift her onto it. We'll carry an end each, like a hammock.'

The little rescue party got under way. With frequent stops to draw breath they negotiated the difficult last lap up the stairs and laid the limp, half-conscious figure on the sofa.

'The first thing to do,' said Florence, wiping her brow, 'is to get these wet clothes off. Patience, bring me one of my flannel nightgowns from the chest of drawers – she's nearer to my size than yours, I think.'

'Is she sick?' Patience asked

'I don't think so. There's no fever, but she's certainly very weak.'

Florence held the wet gown to her nose – 'This is sea water!'

Patience gently inserted the girl's brown arms into the sleeves of her mother's nightdress. Florence took the wet clothes into the kitchen and Patience perched on the arm of a chair and observed the newcomer, who seemed to have sunk into a deep sleep. Her tight brown curls had dried and she'd stopped shivering.

'How old do you think she is?' Patience asked curiously.

'It's hard to say – about fifteen, perhaps.' Florence felt the girl's pulse. 'She seems quite healthy, but it looks as though she'll need to sleep for a while.'

'But what was she doing in the graveyard? And why was she wet? And where are her shoes?'

Florence smiled and shook her head. 'We'll have to wait until she can tell us herself. But she's not without shoes because she's poor – her clothes are beautifully made. And her hands don't look as though she's used to rough work.'

Patience felt she would burst with curiosity as she and her mother sat down to a late and rather dry dinner.

'I wonder what her name is,' she speculated through a mouthful of mashed potato.

'Something that begins with X.T.,' replied Florence, who'd observed these initials embroidered on their guest's underwear.

'You can't have a name beginning with X!' spluttered Patience.

'Patience, please!' remonstrated her mother. 'Ladies don't speak when they're eating!'

Patience was well used to being told what ladies did and did not do. Florence did not regard herself as a snob, but, as a minister's daughter, she was aware that marriage to her beloved carpenter husband had represented a step down the social ladder. Whilst she had never regretted her choice, not for one minute of the past fifteen years, she had resolved that her daughter would be 'nicely brought up'.

Patience sighed. There were so many intriguing questions crying out for answers. But the only person who could answer them was to remain deeply asleep for the next twelve hours. When Patience herself fell asleep that night in the double bed she now shared with her mother, it was to dream of having to carry an impossibly heavy baby up Castle Hill, where Uncle Huw was waiting to present her with a leather-bound tome. But she couldn't read it because all the words consisted of X's.

She awoke suddenly to the smell of soup and the sound of quiet voices from the living-room. Her mother's half of the bed was empty and Patience sat up, feeling cross and left out. She swung her legs over the edge of the bed and lowered her feet onto the cold floorboards. Clasping the knob of the door, she turned it very quietly and, in the dark of the bedroom, stood for a moment taking in the scene that was revealed by the light of the oil lamp on the living-room table, for dawn was only just breaking.

Her mother sat beside the sofa in her nightgown, her hair in two long braids. She was holding the hand of the dark girl, who sat upright, a shawl across her shoulders. The girl looked younger than she had done when she was asleep and seemed altogether slighter, but her voice was deeper than Patience had expected and she spoke very distinctly with a slight singsong accent.

'. . . and when I saw the chapel, I thought there might be someone there who could help me,' Patience heard her say. Florence nodded.

'Patience,' she said, without turning her head, 'come and meet Xanthe. I've been telling her about you.'

So that was her name. Her mother pronounced it so that it sounded like 'Zanthay'. Patience crept into the room, suddenly shy. The girls looked at one another. Patience thought that she had never seen such beautiful, amber eyes. Then she remembered her manners.

'I hope you're feeling better,' she said.

Xanthe smiled and immediately the ice was broken.

'I'm sorry I frightened you in the graveyard,' she said.

'Why were you wet?' Patience asked her. 'Where had you been?'

Xanthe looked at Florence.

'It's a long story, Patience,' her mother said. 'And no wonder Xanthe was so exhausted. She and her mother were trying to swim ashore from a ship that lay at anchor, but they got separated and it seems . . .' – she paused and put an arm around Xanthe – 'it seems that Xanthe's mother may not have managed it.' Patience looked from one to the other. Did her mother mean that Xanthe's mother had drowned?

'Now that Xanthe is with us,' Florence went on, 'she's going to need our love and support.'

Xanthe covered her face with her hands and her shoulders heaved silently, as Florence held her close.

'I know she didn't manage it,' Xanthe whispered. 'I know she didn't!'

Patience gazed dumbly at the girl's bowed head, recalling the conversation in the chandler's shop. The drowned body must have been Xanthe's mother! She felt overwhelmed and helpless. What could she say that could possibly make any difference to this poor girl's grief? At least Patience's father had died in his bed at home with his family around him. Xanthe's mother had died alone and frightened in the cold sea. Tentatively, she placed a hand on Xanthe's arm.

'I'm so sorry, Xanthe,' she said reticently. The words seemed ridiculously inadequate, but Xanthe raised a tear-stained face.

'I . . . I know a bit how it feels,' Patience went on. 'My father died very recently, so we're sad, too.'

Xanthe wiped her eyes on a corner of a blanket and looked from one to the other. She shook her head.

'And now you have me to add to your troubles!' She seemed about to dissolve into fresh tears, but Patience took her two hands in hers.

'You're not a trouble!' she exclaimed. 'You're a new friend! You can stay with us until you're better and then we can take you to where you were going. Where *were* you going? And why did . . .'

'Oh!' Xanthe said, spreading out her hands, 'I

don't know where we were going exactly and oh, it's such a long, long story!'

'In that case,' said Florence, standing up, 'it had better wait until you've had some more rest, I think.'

'Oh, but I'd like to tell it you,' Xanthe said quickly. 'That is, if you don't mind. If . . . if you know more about me, you see, I shan't feel quite so much alone.'

Florence nodded understandingly.

'Why don't you both climb into the big bed and I'll heat up some soup. We can have a breakfast picnic!'

Patience conducted her new friend into the bedroom and plumped the bolsters of the brass bedstead. When Florence came in with mugs of hot soup, the two were sitting side by side beneath the patchwork quilt as if they had known one another all their lives.

The soup was warm and soothing. Florence made herself comfortable at the end of the bed, and as the sun rose slowly over the roofs of Liverpool, Xanthe embarked on a story that was to hold her two listeners spellbound.

3

Escape from 'Rose Lea'

'Our home,' Xanthe began, cupping her hands around the warm mug, 'was a white house called "Rose Lea" on the island of Antigua. It was very big and very beautiful. There were crystal chandeliers in the drawing-room, and in the garden a lake with a fountain and swans.'

'Are you very rich?' Patience asked wide-eyed.

Xanthe shook her head. 'No – we owned nothing of our own. The house belonged to Mr Tresco. Mother and I belonged to him, too. We were slaves.'

'But,' said Patience, who had learnt about slavery at Sunday School and had put a penny a week in the Abolition Society collecting box, 'I thought slaves worked on plantations and got beaten.'

Xanthe nodded. 'Most of Mr Tresco's slaves did work the sugar plantation. And other owners whipped their slaves. But we were very lucky because he never had his workers punished like that. And Mother and I,' Xanthe went on in her measured voice, 'were domestic slaves. We were more valuable than the field slaves because we were skilled.'

Florence and Patience were all attention, their eyes focussed on the slim figure leaning against the pillows. In the space of a few sentences she had transported them from the cramped little Liverpool bedroom to a distant world of which they were only dimly aware.

'When I was born,' Xanthe went on, 'Mother had worked in the dairy at Rose Lea, and when I was very small I learnt to turn the handle of the butter churn and later to make cheese and skim milk. I loved it in the dairy because it was cool and had a lovely, fresh smell, and all the pans and ladles were laid out, shining bright, along the shelves.' Patience nodded. Her father had given just such a description of the dairy at Hafod.

'Then,' Xanthe went on, 'when I was seven, Mother was put in charge of the laundry and she taught me to hem and mend the damaged linen. We nearly alway . . .' Xanthe paused and her voice shook a little, 'we . . . were nearly always allowed to work together.' She wiped the back of her hand across her eyes. Florence passed her a handkerchief.

'Don't go on, Xanthe, if you don't want to,' she said. Xanthe blew her nose.

'I do want to,' she insisted. 'I want you to know all about me because nobody else here does.'

'Then do go on!' urged Patience, fascinated.

'Well,' said Xanthe, 'Mother began to make dresses for Miss Daisy, Mr Tresco's daughter. She was nearly my age – a bit younger – and Mother was allowed to keep the offcuts to make clothes for me.'

'Did she make the dress you came in?' Patience asked, remembering her mother's comments about it. 'Oh, Xanthe,' she added remorsefully, as the girl's eyes brimmed up again, 'I'm sorry!'

'It's alright,' Xanthe said. 'I have to get used to talking about her. And yes, she did make that dress and many more. But most were left behind, except the two that are in my bag on the ship. And if anyone finds them . . .' – her voice grew suddenly agitated – 'and if they see the initials inside, and if they find me . . .' – her speech grew faster – 'then I could be blamed for the death of Captain Manders – and perhaps sent to prison – and – perhaps – hanged!'

She pressed her hands to her face and rocked back and forth in distress.

'Xanthe, what are you talking about?' asked Florence, fearing that the girl was becoming delirious. Xanthe swallowed hard and took a deep breath.

'I will explain,' she said more calmly, 'but . . .'

'But what?' Florence asked, concernedly.

'You are my friends, aren't you?'

'Of course!' Patience exclaimed. 'We won't let anyone harm you, or put you in prison, or hang you, but Xanthe, do tell us what you are talking about! Who is Captain Manders and why is he dead?'

'First,' said Xanthe, 'you must understand that Mr Tresco was one of the better planters. He looked after his slaves and took an interest in them. He even allowed Mr Clark, the pastor, to start a mission school for them. Most slave owners weren't willing for their slaves to learn anything in case it gave them ideas about freedom, but Mr Tresco thought his workers would work better if they were contented.'

'And did you go to the mission school,' Patience asked, curiously.

Xanthe shook her head.

'No. Mr Tresco wanted me to be Miss Daisy's companion because she was an only child. She had a governess, Miss Gray, and we had daily lessons together in the schoolroom at Rose Lea. She taught us French, music and drawing. I liked geography best. Sometimes I helped at the mission school on Saturdays – I loved that. But then . . .' she sighed, 'then everything started to go badly wrong.'

'What sort of wrong?' Patience asked.

'Well – Mr Tresco had inherited the plantation when he was younger from his father and he wasn't very good at it. He left it all to his overseer because he really only wanted to be in his library all day, reading books in Latin and Greek. So when the price of sugar fell, he lost nearly all his money because sugar was all that he grew and a lot of his money was tied up in his slaves. He couldn't sell us without selling the estate because it was against the law, so he became bankrupt and the family left for England very suddenly. But then an even worse thing happened.'

'What?' Patience asked, hugging her knees. Xanthe leant forward.

'Mother overheard Mr Tresco's agent telling the overseer the name of the man who had bought the estate and who was to be our new owner. It was Francis Drummond! That,' said Xanthe, 'was a terrible name for any slave to hear. He was known to be the cruellest planter on the island and beyond it. Mr Tresco bought Mother from Mr Drummond's father when she was eight years old. It was he who had had her branded on the shoulder. Drummond slaves were flogged every day and sometimes they died. As for the women slaves, they had to be pregnant all the time to make more slaves for him – even if they were only twelve.

'Well, as soon as Mother heard this news, she packed two bags and told the housekeeper we were taking some of Miss Daisy's things to St John's to be shipped to England. Then we both went to see Mr Clark, the missionary, at his lodgings. Mother had been allowed to earn a little money of her own from the dressmaking for Mr Tresco's free servants, and over the years she'd managed to save £60.'

Xanthe paused to draw breath and Florence poured her a glass of water from a jug on the marble-topped washstand. 'Mr Clark was just as worried,' Xanthe continued between sips, 'because not only would he be out of a job, but Mr Drummond had the power to arrest him for inciting the slaves to revolt if he had a mind to. Another missionary who had tried to teach the slaves on St Lucia had been hanged on that charge. Well, Mr Clark's lodgings were near to the harbour in St John's, and he used all of his and Mother's savings to persuade the captain of a trading vessel, Captain Manders, to take us to England as passengers. He told the captain that we'd bought our freedom legally (which wasn't true, of course) and Manders pretended to believe him because he wanted the money. He was sailing that very night. So we boarded the ship and went. Just like that. Without saying goodbye to anyone. Well,' Xanthe took another sip of water – 'Mr Clark had a small cabin on the ship – it was called *Pride of the Indies* – but as soon as we set sail, Captain Manders ordered that Mother and I be kept in the hold. All we had was sacking to lie on and we were allowed very little food. If it hadn't been for Mr Clark I think we'd have been given none. It was a dreadful voyage. Almost all of the crew treated us dreadfully and we ran into such storms – it all seemed to go on for ever and so cold!

'Then Mr Clark fell ill with terrible pains in his stomach. Mother was allowed to look after him and she did what she could, but when we were ten days out of Liverpool he died. The captain had him buried at sea in case he'd died of something catching. Mother was very afraid that, with Mr Clark gone, the captain would take us back to Antigua on the return voyage because we had a price on our heads. She said that, because we were both skilled, we were

33

valued at £100 each. So we stayed in the hold and hoped we'd been forgotten and I think – for the most part – we were. There was one member of the crew who put biscuits and a flask of water outside the hatch for us every night secretly. We only ever saw his arm – it had crossed flags tattooed on it. Mother called him our Guardian Angel. We never knew who he was, but without him we'd certainly have died. Even when we were in sight of Liverpool we couldn't dock because we had to wait for the tide to turn, so we weighed anchor offshore.

'That night was terribly stormy and the crew – and Captain Manders – all got terribly drunk. Mother said we were to stay very quiet and not draw attention to ourselves. We crept out of the hold and hid in Mr Clark's empty cabin. The noise was tremendous with the crew roaring, singing and stamping their feet and the gale howling outside. Then suddenly,' – Xanthe paused and gulped – 'suddenly – the cabin door was flung open with a crash and the captain staggered in. He was very drunk and with the pitching of the ship he could hardly stand. He made straight for me and – dragged me to the bunk and forced me down on it.' Xanthe closed her eyes and Florence put a hand on her shoulder.

'Then – Mother managed to pull him away – she was very strong – and they struggled. She was pushing him back towards the door, but he lost his footing and fell, striking the back of his head on a corner of the locker. He lay there, staring up at the ceiling and then his eyes seemed to glaze over. Mother said "I think he's dead".' Xanthe swallowed. 'Then she said that we must make a plan and act very quickly before the body was discovered.

'The gale seemed to have subsided and we could see the lights of the harbour quite clearly, so we decided to try to swim ashore. Mother said that, if we got separated, we were each to wait for the other by the green light to the right of the harbour. Then, if the other hadn't appeared in an hour, we were to look for a church or chapel and seek help from the minister. She said Mr Clark had told her that, once we were ashore, we would be free people and not slaves any more.' Xanthe spoke quite calmly now, but she shook slightly.

'Mother asked for God's blessing. We took off our shoes, tied up our skirts and slid down a rope at the side of the hull. The water was terribly, terribly cold – and the harbour was much further away than we'd thought. Staying together was too difficult – it took all our strength just to stay afloat. I was lucky because I saw a piece of something – it looked like cork – and I hung on to it and paddled with my feet, and after ages and ages I got to the quay.' Xanthe sank back against the pillows.

'You know the rest,' she said.

The three sat in silence for a while, Florence and Patience overwhelmed by what they had heard. Then Florence asked, 'What was your mother's name, Xanthe?'

'Hannah,' Xanthe said. 'Hannah Tresco.'

Starlings chattered on the roof outside the window. Then Xanthe spoke quietly.

'Do you think,' she said, 'that I shall be wanted for murder?'

4

A Solution

Florence's reply came a little too promptly.

'Of course not!' she said briskly. 'You mustn't think such thoughts!' but her troubled face belied the reassurance. The girl's story had touched her deeply, but she was beginning to wonder why, when she had just succeeded in overcoming one difficulty, Fate had placed another at her door – and one that she had no idea how to resolve.

The new difficulty was gazing at her intensely, clearly waiting for her to enlarge on her reply. Patience looked from one to the other, her knees drawn up tightly under her chin. A thought was taking shape in her mind, but she dared not utter it – at least not yet. Florence moved over to the window.

'We need advice,' she said, drawing back the curtain and speaking half to herself. 'We need to know what Xanthe's position is legally, and then we need to find her somewhere to live where she'll be properly cared for.'

'I'm able to work!' Xanthe said quickly. 'I know how to do a lot of things!'

Morning sunlight filled the room and Patience

noticed how pretty she was with her pale amber eyes fixed on Florence's face. It was unfair, she thought, that brown-skinned people seldom seemed to have spots or freckles.

'That's why,' Florence said, 'it's so important no one takes advantage of you and why . . .'

She was interrupted by a sudden, sharp knock on the outer door. Her hand flew to her mouth.

'Mr Morris the minister!' she cried in dismay, 'come for the coach ticket money – and me in my nightgown!' She took a shawl from a hook behind the door and threw it across her shoulders. 'Stay in here for the moment, both of you – Mr Morris will surely know how to help us!'

The girls heard the bolt of the front door being shot back, followed by the sound of a man's voice in the living-room.

'Mr Morris is the minister of Zion Chapel – the one where I found you,' Patience explained, jumping off the bed and unashamedly placing her ear to the door crack. 'They're talking about us,' she declared after a moment, 'but I can't make out what they're saying.'

'Why has he come?' Xanthe asked. Patience sighed and climbed back onto the bed.

'He's going to take me to Wales,' she said gloomily, and went on to explain the reasons for the trip and the new lives she and her mother were soon to lead.

'So you'll be going away,' Xanthe said sadly.

'But not until I know you're going to be alright!'

Patience answered quickly. 'If Mother's found a job for herself, I'm sure she'd be able to find one for you with all the different things you know how to do. As for being wanted for murder' – Patience's brow crinkled in disbelief – 'how could you be, when you haven't even killed anyone?'

'But it will look as if I have!' Xanthe said, leaning forward, 'with Captain Manders lying dead on the cabin floor and Mother and me jumping ship. And now that Mother's dead, there'll only be me to blame for it!'

'No there won't!' Patience declared. 'They'll think it was an accident, of course, which it was!'

Xanthe looked at her doubtfully.

'Just you wait until you meet Mr Morris,' Patience went on, 'he'll stop you worrying – I know he will!'

'Meet him!' Xanthe said in alarm, 'but I've nothing to wear!'

Patience jumped off the bed and tugged open the wardrobe door.

'I'm nearly five foot,' she said. 'How tall are you?'

'I don't know.' Xanthe joined Patience in front of the wardrobe mirror and the two stood back to back.

'You're taller than me, but I'm fatter than you,' Patience observed accurately, 'but you might just . . .' She dived into the wardrobe and began to rummage, emerging tousle-haired, clutching a gingham dress in green check. 'This was Mother's – she was going to pass it on to Mrs Brinthorpe's niece. Try it on, Xanthe!' Xanthe struggled out of the voluminous nightgown and slipped the dress over her head.

'Perfect!' Patience cried, delighted, buttoning up the back.

'Too long, though,' Xanthe said, looking down.

'Mm . . . yes. But I think there are some pins . . .' Patience opened a small drawer in the washstand. 'Stand still.' She knelt and began pinning up the extra length. 'I'm not as good at this as Mother is – nor as your mother was, either,' she added, remembering the grey dress, drying in the kitchen with its neatly embroidered initials.

'Why,' she asked through a mouthful of pins, 'did your mother call you Xanthe?'

'She didn't,' Xanthe answered. 'Mr Tresco did. He liked to name all the new slave babies himself – he did it alphabetically. Mother said that when she took me to see him in his library – he was never anywhere else – he took a big tome down from the shelf and looked up an "X" name in it. Then he wrote down the name and what it meant on a piece of paper and gave it to Mother – which wasn't a lot of use because she couldn't read. But she kept it and gave it to me once I could.'

'And what does it mean?'

Xanthe screwed up her eyes in an effort of recollection and recited 'Xanthe: one of the eight daughters of Oceanus, god of the ocean. Reputed to have the power to save sailors from death.'

'Goodness!' said Patience, impressed. She took the pins out of her mouth. 'I wish I'd been named after the daughter of a god, instead of after a virtue – and a boring one at that!'

Suddenly the bedroom door opened and Florence entered, looking noticeably more relaxed.

'Mr Morris would like to see you both before he goes,' she said, smiling at Xanthe's attire, which was receiving its final pin.

'But I'm in my nightgown and we're both barefoot!' Patience protested.

'So that makes three of us! Come along – Mr Morris won't mind. He has daughters of his own!' She shepherded them into the living-room as a stout, bespectacled figure came towards them, arms outstretched in greeting.

'Good morning, good morning!' he cried jovially, placing a podgy hand on the girls' shoulders.

'So this is Xanthe! I am only sorry, my dear, that we meet under such very sad circumstances. Mrs Penry has told me your remarkable story. And to think that you sought refuge at my chapel and I was not there to assist you! But this young lady saved the situation, I hear!' He beamed down at Patience.

He led the girls to the sofa, positioned himself between them and cleared his throat. 'Mrs Penry and I,' he began, 'have arrived at a plan. It may not be quite ideal, but we hope, Xanthe, that it will provide you with a little security – at least for the time being.'

'I'm very much obliged to you,' said Xanthe, politely.

'I believe,' the minister went on, 'that your anxieties about being held accountable for the demise of Captain Manders are quite groundless, for who could bring such a charge? Certainly not the crew, and certainly not the ship's owners, for they know nothing of your existence. No – if you are in any danger, it would be from elsewhere.'

'From where?' Patience asked, anxiously.

The Reverend Morris pursed his lips.

'Liverpool,' he said, 'is full of rogues who could seek to profit from Xanthe's illegal sale. My involvement with the Anti-Slavery Movement gives me some knowledge of the situation, you see. And whilst trading in slaves (although, alas, not owning them) was made illegal in Britain some twenty-six years ago, profits are still to be made from the kidnap and sale of skilled slaves to the Americas. The risk is small,' he added quickly, as Xanthe's face became agitated, 'but we cannot afford to ignore it. And that is why' – he patted her arm reassuringly – 'we have made our plan to remove you to a place of safety for a while.' He rose and took up a commanding position before the fireplace. Patience held her breath, hardly daring to hope for what might be coming next. Florence, seated at the table, gave her a suspicion of a wink.

'Young Patience, as we know,' said Mr Morris, 'is shortly to travel to Wales to reside at her aunt and uncle's farm. We think it best, Xanthe, if you accompany her. Mrs Penry will write to her brother-in-law and – God willing – the end of the summer will see the passage of the anti-slavery bill at last. After that – we shall think again!'

Xanthe's face relaxed into a smile of relief as Patience, with a squeal of joy, clasped her in a pincer-like hug of delight. Her secret hopes had been realised!

Suddenly, the journey to Wales had been transformed from an ordeal into an adventure. She glanced at the leather-bound trunk, standing open by the piano, the sight of which had filled her heart with foreboding. Now she pictured it strapped to the roof of The Holyhead Flyer as she and Xanthe bowled along the highway, scattering chickens and admiring onlookers! Florence was smiling, too, but held up a restraining hand, for Mr Morris was still speaking.

'. . . and our committee, I know, will be more than happy to meet the cost of the additional coach ticket. Which means,' he added, pulling a brass watch from his waistcoat pocket, 'that I must be on my way to the Gascoyne Arms to reserve our seats!'

Florence rose and held out the minister's gloves and hat.

'I feel quite excited myself!' he owned, adjusting his hat in the mantelpiece mirror, 'at the prospect of travelling with two charming young ladies in six days' time!' He turned to Xanthe and his face became grave. 'My dear, we have not forgotten that all this is taking place in the midst of your grief and loss. We shall, I hope, join in prayer for your mother before we depart.'

'Thank you,' Xanthe said. 'And thank you for what you have done for me!'

Florence followed the little man out through the door and down the stairs.

Patience beamed at Xanthe in delight.

'I don't feel frightened now that you're coming too,' she said. 'We can learn about farming together!'

Xanthe smiled back at her, relaxed for the first time. She looked around.

'Can I have a needle and thread?' she asked. 'These pins are sticking in my legs!' Patience darted to the sideboard and lifted Florence's heavy sewing box onto the table. She watched as Xanthe's nimble fingers threaded the needle and began to sew. Taking a small tin from the sideboard drawer, she said cautiously, 'I know you're the daughter of a god, but if I make you an offering of a piece of fudge – would you darn my stockings for me?'

Xanthe looked at her sideways.

'I might,' she said, popping the offering into her mouth. 'But then' – she swallowed and her eyes twinkled – 'I might not!' Patience launched a ball of wool at her friend's head. When Florence entered, the two were pelting each other with mending, as they dodged around the room, squealing.

'Sshh!' – she held up a warning finger. Silence fell. And for the first time in weeks, the sound of the Brinthorpe broom banging on the ceiling below was heard again at 7a Jamaica Street.

5

Leaders and Backers

Andrew Rookwood, coachman of The Holyhead
Flyer, paced the yard of the Gascoyne Arms,
thwacking a whip against his leather gaiters and
booming directions. Snorting and clattering their
hooves, the two 'leaders' and the two 'backers' were
backed up to the waiting coach. Stable-lads scurried,
post-boys in their velvet livery strutted and
passengers stood, singly or in groups, at a respectful
distance, mindful that this was no ordinary coach,
but the Holyhead Mail, for which turnpike gates
flew open at the first note of the horn, and which
waited for no one.

Mrs Morris, wife of the minister, sat on a bench at
the back of the inn yard, a daughter on either side
and her husband pacing before her. Her face, which
resembled that of an anxious chicken, relaxed into a
smile, as three poke bonnets appeared around the
archway of the yard entrance. Pink-faced, Florence,
Patience and Xanthe wove their way through the
throng, followed, breathlessly, by Mr Brinthorpe's
'boy', pushing their trunk in a wooden handcart.
Greetings were exchanged, Xanthe introduced, and

compliments proffered by the Miss Morrises on the elegance of Patience's and Xanthe's bonnets, which Florence had sat up until two in the morning to complete.

When Patience had emerged, bleary-eyed, from the bedroom at six o'clock to behold the very first, grown-up poke bonnet of her dreams, Florence had feared that her cries of delight would awaken the neighbourhood. The bonnets were of ruched silk, Patience's blue and Xanthe's green, with fashionable ribbons and a small rosette in a darker shade tucked alluringly inside each brim. Patience had tried hers on instantly, standing on the coal box to see into the mirror, and refusing to remove it for an instant, so that dressing had to be done from the feet up. Twice, on the long walk from Jamaica Street, she had almost fallen headlong, so compelling was the reflection of this newly adult headwear in the passing windows.

Now Patience surveyed the inn yard, certain that it contained more noise, more smells and more people than any equivalent space in the world. Conversation had to be conducted *fortissimo* and a man selling caged linnets shouted that they could all sing *Rule Britannia*.

Patience's attention was caught by a tall young man leaning against the doorpost of the inn's kitchen. His complexion was weather-beaten, he wore several days' beard, and he stared fixedly at Xanthe from beneath a broad-brimmed hat, which partly obscured his face. Xanthe, in conversation with the elder Miss Morris, was clearly unaware of his gaze. The side of his face that was visible was rather good looking, and Patience felt a hint of envy at the rapt attention that Xanthe was commanding.

'Oh my!' cried the Miss Morrises in unison, clapping their hands to their ears, as the guard gave an impromptu flourish on the horn 'to check it was working', before tucking it with studied nonchalance inside his jacket, well pleased with the stir he had created. Patience saw that Mrs Morris was speaking to her.

'. . . wonderful to be staying in the country! Where exactly is your uncle's farm?'

'It's called Hafod,' Patience replied, raising her voice in order to be heard, 'and it's near the village of Abercroes, twenty-six miles from Ruthin. We change coaches at Chester and Uncle Huw will meet us at Ruthin.'

Suddenly she sensed that someone was standing close behind her and, turning, saw the tall young man in the hat move swiftly away, tossing a jacket over his shoulder with a sunburnt hand that had a grey, ragged bandage wound around the wrist. He disappeared into the crowd and Patience felt a moment of misgiving. But the incident quickly became forgotten as an impressive figure in a caped greatcoat, whom she had taken to be the Duke of Wellington's twin brother, strode up and Andrew Rookwood addressed Mr Morris brusquely.

'Inside or out?'

'These ladies inside,' Mr Morris gestured to the two girls, 'myself outside.'

'Luggage?'

An army of stable-boys sought to out-bawl each other with yells of 'Steady her up!' 'This end first!' 'Up she goes!' as the trunk was hoisted onto the coach roof and the coachman roared at the boys stationed at the horses' heads to hold them steady.

Patience felt her stomach suddenly lurch as the moment of parting drew near. They had exchanged their final hugs and messages before leaving home and Patience had requested no public kisses. Xanthe took her arm and Mrs Morris's voice joined a chorus of last-minute advice as the passengers climbed aboard.

Unable to look her mother in the face, Patience reached out and squeezed Florence's hand in a last, nutcracker grasp before stumbling into the dark interior of the coach and its enveloping smell of leather and straw. She collapsed heavily onto the horsehair seat as figures took their place around her. She could only stare fixedly in the direction of her boots, praying that her tightly-clenched jaw would not allow her chin to quiver.

The coach swayed as Andrew Rookwood heaved himself onto the driving seat, and Patience was only dimly aware of the commotion outside as, at a cry of 'Run wiv'em, boys!' the horses darted forward.

The horn sounded triumphantly, the wheels grated

over the cobbles and out onto the high road, leaving behind a flotilla of waving hats and handkerchiefs and a receding roar of excitement. Gradually the noise resolved itself into the steady beat of sixteen hooves and the gentle creak of leather and springs. It was not until they had clattered over Runcorn Bridge that Patience's eyes unmisted enough to reveal the outline of her boots and she felt able to relax her rigid back. Xanthe breathed with relief as her friend removed the fingernails that had been embedded in her forearm. They exchanged wan smiles from within the hoods of their bonnets and Patience began cautiously to observe her surroundings. They were, indeed, travelling at speed – backwards in Patience's and Xanthe's case – and as the broad sandbanks of the Mersey estuary moved steadily away to their left, to be replaced by faster-moving cottages and haystacks closer to hand, Patience began to experience the exhilaration of coach travel. Once clear of Frodsham village, with its clamouring geese and cheering boys, the guard sounded a flourish on the horn to clear the road ahead and the team broke into a gallop. The carriage swayed, cottagers in smocks and straw hats waved their rakes and Patience longed to join the passengers on the roof so that she could wave back. Glancing at the two passengers opposite, she felt at a loss to comprehend their indifference. One of them, a beautiful young lady with golden ringlets and a superior expression, held before her face a book entitled *Pensées des*

Philosophes Français and moved her eyes from it only to stare disdainfully at Patience's hand-knitted black stockings. Her own stockings were of white silk, but Patience noticed with satisfaction that her bonnet had no rosette. A man next to her, whom Patience took to be the young lady's father, crunched peppermints loudly from behind *The Times*. Patience turned to look at Xanthe. She felt neglectful of her friend, so absorbed had she been in the emotion of departure and the novelty of coach travel. Xanthe was resting her head against the back of the seat, her eyes closed, looking more relaxed than Patience had ever seen her. The slight furrow between her eyebrows, present even at happier moments, had disappeared and with every mile covered, a weight seemed to slip further from her shoulders. Patience was aware of how much more Xanthe had had to fear during the past week than she, and of how much more poignant her loss had been. Yet she had found a way to join in with everyday tasks and they had laughed – and sometimes cried together. Patience had come to rely on her new friend and, after only eight days, found it hard to imagine being without her.

Xanthe's eyes opened and, as she turned her head to look out of the carriage window, they grew round with surprise. Patience followed her gaze and her jaw dropped. Upside-down outside the half-open window hung the top half of Mr Morris, beaming broadly, like Humpty Dumpty in mid-fall.

'Is all well within, ladies?' he enquired genially, his hair flying in the wind. Patience, sensing the superior young lady's gaze, was too embarrassed to reply.

'Yes, thank you,' said Xanthe hastily, 'we are quite comfortable.'

'Sit upright, please, sir!' boomed Andrew Rookwood. 'You'm unbalancing the 'osses!'

To Patience's relief, Mr Morris withdrew, apologising. But no sooner had he done so, than the handle of his umbrella was lowered and tapped insistently on the glass. A piece of paper was attached to it, which Patience, fervently wishing that Mr Morris would fall off at the next bend, was obliged to retrieve.

'The coachman informs us,' she read aloud, 'that we are ahead of time and, barring accidents, will have broken the record of The Shrewsbury Wonder by the time we arrive at the Red Lion at Chester!'

'By George – so that's what he's about!' the peppermint cruncher cried. 'Sit tight, m'dear!' The young lady raised her book and her nose an inch higher and Patience reached for Xanthe's hand under cover of the shawl as the carriage rocked more violently and the coachman's voice roared abuse at a startled farmer, whose horse sprang to the verge in the nick of time.

As they sped through the last open toll-gate to the customary cheers, the guard shouted 'Chester ahead!' and the team was forced to slacken its pace

51

as other traffic converged upon the high road. Fields gave way to cottages, cottages to houses and houses to shops and taverns. Andrew Rookwood's voice, accompanied by frequent blasts on the guard's horn, cajoled, swore and chivvied the population to get out of the way. As they clattered into the yard of the Red Lion, a mighty cheer went up: they'd broken the record! Their own record! The Shrewsbury Wonder's record! Everybody's record!

Crumpled and stiff, the passengers descended to be shaken by the hand or slapped on the back, according to gender. Andrew Rookwood's considerable bulk was carried in triumph around the yard on the shoulders of the pot-boys, and money was seen to be changing hands amongst the taproom regulars. The leaders and backers, who wanted nothing so much as a draught of water and a bucket of oats, were subjected to more pats and slaps until their driver ordered them to be led away, sweating and steaming, to be rubbed down.

An irresistible smell of roast beef wafted from the dining-room and past Patience's nose, but with dinner at three shillings and sixpence a head, Mr Morris led the way to a bench at the end of the yard, where he set about unpacking a parcel of bread, cheese and pickled herrings, motioning Xanthe and Patience to join him.

'Enjoy your repast!' commanded Mr Morris. 'The Ruthin coach will not arrive for half an hour.'

The pickled herrings were delicious. Patience ate

four, having been too nervous for breakfast. She settled down to watch the preparations for The Flyer's next stage, remarking, as a fresh team of four were led past them to be harnessed up, that this was a pleasure denied to the expensive passengers in the dining-room.

'Self-sufficiency is a great blessing!' declared Mr Morris. He moved his spectacles to the end of his nose and began to peruse an oily copy of *The Methodist Chronicle* that had been wrapped around the pickled herrings. The sight of the newspaper jogged Xanthe's memory.

'Mr Morris,' she ventured quietly, 'a gentleman on the coach was reading *The Times*, and I noticed something about . . .' Her voice sank to a whisper and her head joined the minister's behind the open newspaper. Patience drew near to listen. Poke bonnets were advantageous when it came to confidences.

'Indeed, you are quite right!' Mr Morris was saying in a low voice. 'We have great hopes. A bill for the abolition of slavery is, yet again, being placed before Parliament. We have had many setbacks, and must be prepared for more. Mr Wilberforce is a dying man, and I pray that, this time, we may succeed!'

'What will it mean?' Patience asked, joining them behind the newspaper.

'Why,' the minister replied, 'it will make three quarters of a million people in the British West Indies free from bondage for the first time! And it will remove from ex-slaves the world over the ever-present fear of being kidnapped for gain. Then,' he went on earnestly, 'our work will really begin – teachers and missionaries will be wanted out there as never before!'

'Oh! Do you think . . .?' Xanthe placed a hand timidly on Mr Morris's arm, but they were interrupted by a roar from Andrew Rookwood, emerging from the saloon.

'Holyhead passengers, please!' he bellowed with his mouth full.

'I will keep you closely informed, never fear!' Mr Morris pressed Xanthe's hand reassuringly.

Diners bustled importantly out of the inn. This time, Patience was able to savour all the excitement of the coach's departure. She stood on the bench to wave as, once again, the horn sounded, the yellow wheels rolled and the record-breaking Flyer disappeared in a cloud of dust and din.

'I can't decide,' she mused, climbing down, 'which is the more exciting – a coach arriving, or a coach departing.'

'A coach departing, I think,' said Xanthe, 'because it's the beginning of something.'

'In that case,' pronounced the minister, standing up and brushing the crumbs from his waistcoat, 'our beginning is about to arrive!'

6

A Change of Plan

Dear Mother,

It was only this very morning that we said goodby, but things have taken an altergether unexpected turn, so I am using some pages from the notebook you gave me to write to you. There is about an inch of candle left and Xanthe is asleep so I will start at the beginning. The male coach went very fast and we thought the men on the roof were going to fall off but they didn't. I felt sorry for the horses who were swetting. The next coach was a lot slower it was full of farmers' wives with baskets of chickens.

55

They spoke welsh (not the chickens) which Xanthe hadn't heard before and I could understand quite a lot of it The best part was that we were allowed to sit on the roof! The coachman said the Holyhead Flyer turns over a lot or else breaks a pole all to win wagers, which we were thankful we did not know. Well when we arrived at Ruthin there was no sign of Uncle Huw. We waited and waited and then the landlord who had seen us all along said was one of us Miss Penry and I said yes I was and he gave me a letter. It was from Motreb and it was in welsh but Mr Morris helped me with it. It said Uncle Huw had fallen out of the hayloft and hurt his back so badly he cannot move so we were to stay here tonight and tell the landlord who we were and Uncle Huw will settle when he is better. We are to leave early in the morning with Mr William Gwyn the drover who is taking a drove of sheep to Newtown and passing by Hafod. She said he is a gŵr dodfaw (a good man I think) and we will be safe with him so you are not to worry Mother. Mr Morris says we will not arrive before Thursday because the sheep will lose wait if they try to cover more than sixteen miles a day. We shall have to leave our trunk here until Uncle Huw comes I suppose. It could not be carried up to our room because they do not have a boy so we are to sleep in our underware. Mr Morris had bread, ham and tea sent up and went to his engagement. He said we were to bolt the door and not go out until he comes for us in the morning. We are above the taproom and there is a lot of noise and smells coming up through the not holes in the floor. The candle is spluttering so I must end. When I next write it will be from Hafod. Goodnight dear mother. Write soon. Your loving Patience.

P.S. I will give this to Mr Morris to send.

Patience folded the pages and slid off the bed to tuck the letter in her boot. The loud voices below began to drift away. Lifting a corner of the curtain she could just make out the form of the last customer making his unsteady way down the street, a little dog at his heels. She blew out the candle and applied a damp finger to the wick before sliding into the knobbly bed next to Xanthe.

* * *

Early morning sunlight was already glinting between the houses as the Reverend Morris made his way to the Drovers' Arms, the shadow of his rotund form and briskly swinging arms moving beside him. A confusion of voices drifted from the direction of the inn, as farmers and drovers congregated to argue prices, strike bargains and settle dues. He pushed open the door and the hum became a roar.

'Oh! I wish he'd hurry up,' cried Patience in the bedroom. 'I can't wait to learn if we're to ride real, live ponies!'

'Well, we won't be riding dead ones, for sure,' smiled Xanthe at the window. 'And you won't have to wait long – he's here!' But it was a good ten minutes before a brisk knock allowed them to draw back the bolt of the oaken door.

'I have been detained in conversation!' declared the minister, to their no great surprise. 'But porridge and tea await – follow me!'

He led the girls downstairs and through a barrage of noise, tobacco smoke, tankard-clutching fists and gesticulating pipe-stems to the haven of a large inglenook beside the fire. A woman with a polished face served them porridge in wooden bowls.

'Cups and saucers for young ladies!' she pronounced with pride, glancing with interest at Xanthe's brown face. 'Are you travelling far?'

'To a farm near Abercroes,' Patience told her, 'with Mr Gwyn the drover.'

'With William Gwyn! You'll be safe enough with him!'

'Do you know him?'

'Like my own father. He's a remarkable man. It's said that he can hear the grass growing in the fields and the wool sprouting on the sheep's backs!'

Mr Morris had migrated towards a tall man whose face, beneath its mane of greying hair, looked as if it had been chiselled out of rock. Over an assortment of woollen garments he wore a long, linen smock and he towered above the farmers who clamoured for his attention. Transactions were being undertaken and he made frequent entries in a well-thumbed notebook. When Mr Morris succeeded in gaining an audience, William Gwyn had to bend to hear his words. Straightening up, he turned and gazed majestically in the direction of the two girls in the corner. The rest of the room seemed to turn and gaze likewise, and Patience and Xanthe buried their faces in their teacups. At last there was a movement in the centre of the room. A group of drinkers around the door fell back and William Gwyn swept out. Mr Morris beckoned the girls to follow.

Out in the yard they found William Gwyn supervising a group of herdsmen in the art of soaping the soles of their thick woollen socks.

'A necessary practice,' Mr Morris explained. 'It prevents blisters and waterproofs the socks should the boots leak.'

William Gwyn approached and the minister made the introductions. The drover solemnly shook each girl by the hand.

'Mr Penry of Hafod is an old acquaintance. You will be safe with me.' Like everything else about him, William Gwyn's voice was impressive, deep and resonant.

'Thank you,' Patience said. She didn't feel quite brave enough to ask about the possibility of riding.

'We shall be driving eight hundred head of sheep,' the drover went on, 'and I have six herdsmen and twelve dogs to help me.' He fixed them with his gaze as he spoke, as if to emphasise the gravity of the undertaking. 'It will be a long walk, but we go slowly and we stop every three miles for the beasts to graze so that they don't lose weight. I won't have a spare pony for you to start with, but we shall pick one up a few miles along the way.'

'Mr Gwyn hopes to cover sixteen miles today,' put in Mr Morris, 'and to stop at Maes Coch farm where you'll be given a bed. You should reach Hafod by tomorrow afternoon.'

Sixteen miles! Patience had never walked more than two in her life. She glanced at Xanthe, but her friend seemed unperturbed and gestured across the yard where the drover was tapping the top of the mounting block with his stick.

'Sit here, please,' he said. Obediently the girls climbed the stone steps and sat down gingerly on the broad stone platform as the drover drew a long length of hessian from a pocket in his capacious breeches and proceeded to wrap it around one of Patience's boots.

'Oh!' she exclaimed in dismay, 'I'm sure I shan't need that!'

William Gwyn fixed her with a steely gaze.

'If you are consigned to my care, Miss Penry, you will do as you are told,' he asserted, deftly fastening each parcelled foot with string and tucking in the ends. Patience submitted meekly, and, when Xanthe's feet had received similar treatment, both girls slid to the ground.

Drover and herdsmen pulled on broad-brimmed hats and led the way out of the yard and along a narrow lane that ran behind the main street. Patience felt thankful that the way was secluded. She was acutely conscious of the contrast between her elegant bonnet and her sack-bound feet.

'When I was a lad,' mused the minister, walking beside them, 'I idolised the drovers! They were hard men – but it takes a deal of skill to handle three hundred or more head of cattle all the way from Beaumaris to Smithfield! They knew every inch of the way and everyone on it. And when it came to news – if the price of butter had risen, a new fashion had been introduced, an election lost or a battle won, the drovers were the first to know! But listen!' – he put a hand to his ear – 'we're approaching the sheep pens!'

Under a group of oaks ahead they could see a herdsman saddling some stocky, mountain ponies. They were surrounded by a collection of small, sharp-eared dogs and suddenly they were at the edge of the fold. As far as the eye could see, there were sheep and the air vibrated with their cries.

Patience realised with a shock that it was almost time to say goodbye to the minister. As the herdsmen moved towards their mounts Mr Morris placed his hands on their shoulders in a gesture that had become familiar to both of them.

'And now I must commit you to the good care of Mr Gwyn. But I hope to visit you at Hafod before too long.'

'Do you?' Patience looked up at him. He had become a father figure and now he seemed like a last link with the known world.

'But of course! I shall be there long before the swallows depart – you'll see. I shall miss you both far too much to leave it any longer. Besides, I have a commitment to Miss Xanthe to keep her in touch with developments!' Crossing to William Gwyn, he shook him warmly by the hand, then quickly turned and set off along the lane to Ruthin without glancing back. Patience drew a sleeve across her eyes.

'We're really on our own now,' she observed.

'Neither of us is on our own!' Xanthe declared. 'I've got you and you've got me!'

Patience smiled wanly. 'I can't imagine how I'd be feeling if you weren't with me!'

William Gwyn opened the gate of the fold, and as the two leading herdsmen moved off on their ponies, a great stream of bawling sheep poured down the trackway, the little corgis darting at their heels. William Gwyn approached the girls.

'It will take a while for the fold to empty,' he said. 'I shall ride at the back and you must always stay in front of me. If you want to stop, you must let me know.' His tone was gentler now and he gave each of them a reassuring pat on the back.

The way ahead had become an undulating sea of woolly backs. The bracken tips along the banks gleamed emerald in the morning sun, and Patience began to feel that they were part of a great enterprise. William Gwyn was already in the saddle. Tilting back his head, he let out a long call in his deep, resonant voice: 'Heiptre Ho-o-o!' The cry was taken up by each of the herdsmen in turn and echoed down the valley as they moved forward. Surrounding farmers were being warned to keep their beasts out of the way. The drove had begun.

Patience and Xanthe gathered up their skirts. And so, with the sun at their backs and their shadows before them, they set off in the direction of the distant hills.

7

'Heiptre Ho!'

Gradually the sheep's voices fell silent until the only sounds were the occasional calls of the herdsmen to their dogs and the ripple of innumerable hooves on the turf. Between the moving flock and the distant hills lay a pattern of colour: fields of hay and barley, green copses and clumps of yellow gorse advanced and receded behind them as they progressed, but the blue hills below the skyline seemed as far away as ever.

Patience had heard and read about the countryside, but the feeling of freedom and openness, the air and lightness all around her – that was something new. She turned to Xanthe.

'Is it different from Antigua?' Xanthe nodded.

'Everything seems bigger. The trees are not the same. And the sky's a different kind of blue.' Patience was on the point of asking about the different kind of blue when the clink of metalled hoof on a stone reminded her of William Gwyn's presence just behind them. She wasn't sure how much he knew about Xanthe or how much it would be safe for him to know. She turned her attention to a ewe which had strayed up the bank to sample a buttercup. One of the herdsmen had given them each a stout hazel stick and Patience found that a tap with this on the erring, woolly bottom was enough to return it to the path. It was all very purposeful and satisfying. The sun was directly above them now. Her legs were beginning to ache and her clothes to stick to her back.

Rounding a bend, the path entered a grove of oak trees and the way descended steeply. The branches closed above their heads and they could hear the gurgle and splash of running water. The going became soft and the sheep were trampling the mud into a morass. The girls began to appreciate the protection of the canvas on their boots. Soon even that became inadequate as the pockets of thick mud deepened.

William Gwyn reined in his pony and dismounted.

'We shall be crossing the river now,' he announced. 'So you must ride and I will walk.' His mount began drawing in great draughts of water from a brown puddle. In quick succession the girls felt themselves borne aloft and placed one behind the other on the broad saddle. They might have been so much thistledown in the drover's powerful grasp. He pulled up the unwilling pony's head, and they followed the sheep into the racing water.

A blanket of cold air rose up around them. Patience held tightly to the front of the saddle as Xanthe grasped her around the waist. The flock was surging ahead, half swimming, half clambering amongst the smooth boulders, their clamouring voices merging with the roar of the torrent and the cries of the herdsmen urging them on.

For Patience the excitement of being on horseback for the first time was tempered by the fear of the pony losing its foothold and plunging them in. The drover's face beside her was impassive as he guided the pony first upstream then down, weaving amongst the rocks and knowing just where to avoid the deep potholes. He was up to his thighs in the water, which almost lapped at Xanthe's feet, but he seemed indifferent to his sodden garments. At last he drew the pony towards a flat shelf of gravel and dry land. A corgi who had been swept downstream came hurtling breathlessly through the gorse bushes to join them. Just as Patience was beginning to enjoy the sensation of riding without any of its hazards, it was time to dismount. There was a suspicion of a twinkle in William Gwyn's eye as he lifted them down.

'You did well. The crossing can be rough. I lost a steer there last year.' He grasped the hem of his smock and twisted it into a knot to wring out the water. 'We shall be climbing now until we reach Bryn Glas. Then we shall rest and you will have your own pony from then on.' Patience shot a gleeful glance at Xanthe. 'This is sheep farming country,' he went on, 'so in a while we shall have to begin the calling again. If any of the local sheep got into our flock they'd be lost to their owners for sure.' He flicked his mount with a stick and Xanthe extended an arm to pull Patience up the slope. All their breath was needed for the ascent, but once clear of the trees the climb became gentler.

'Have – you – ever – ridden – before?' Patience gasped.

'I used to ride with Miss Daisy,' Xanthe answered, grasping the branch of a sycamore to haul herself up the gradient, 'but it was always trotting around and around the gravel drive – never going anywhere.' Patience tried to picture the scene, reflecting that there seemed to be few things that Xanthe, despite her slave status, had not done.

William Gwyn was waiting for them at the top of the slope and they fell in in front of him.

'Heiptre Hoi!' he sang out and again the call was taken up by all twelve of the herdsmen. When the track became level and the going easier, the drover touched Patience on the arm and pointed with his switch towards a farmhouse, just visible behind three pine trees.

'Bryn Glas,' he said. 'When you see pine-trees growing next to a farmhouse like that, you know there is grazing for beasts and rest for drovers!' He kicked his pony into a trot and rode on to meet the farmer who was already helping to herd the sheep into their enclosure. The ponies, unsaddled, took long draughts from a stone trough in front of the house and a group of women and children surrounded the herdsmen, questioning them in excited Welsh voices.

The last of the flock secured, William Gwyn followed the stocky farmer across the yard, bending low as he entered the darkness of the house. Xanthe and Patience sank down on the grass in the shade of the fir-trees, leaning their backs against a cool, lichen-spattered boulder.

'I shan't walk another step!' Patience groaned. She longed to release her aching feet from her boots, but felt unconfident about retying the elaborate sacking arrangement, particularly as it was inside a solid casing of dried mud.

Two brown-eyed little girls approached shyly, carrying pitchers of bubbly milk for the 'ladies *bach*.' They placed their burden carefully on the ground and stood back to observe the newcomers. The elder girl had bare legs and wooden clogs, but the little one was barefoot.

'What are your names?' Xanthe asked them.

'*Dim Saesneg*,' replied the elder one, shaking her head – 'No English.' They swayed back and forth self-consciously, unable to converse, but unwilling to leave the fascinating spectacle before them. Xanthe untied the strings of her bonnet and placed it on the head of the smaller child, who thrust her neck forward delightedly for the strings to be tied beneath her tiny chin. Squealing, she raced back towards the farmhouse, colliding with her mother, a sturdy woman in a canvas apron, who wore her black hair in a thick plait around her head. She carried oatcakes and cheese on a wooden board. Patience rose to help

68

her, keeping a wary eye on half a dozen geese who stalked behind.

'*Diolch yn fawr.*' Beckoning with a reddened arm, the woman called to the herdsmen who lay around the gateway to the fold, their hats over their faces.

'*Dewch i gael bwyd!*' – 'Come and eat!' One by one they rose stiffly and approached the laden board. Xanthe, who had been enjoying a game of chase around the farmyard, rejoined Patience under the trees, her bonnet retrieved. She fanned her face with it as the little ones danced around her, delighting in the novelty of a visitor who played games. With a clap of her strong hands their mother shooed them away.

'Enchoy your meal,' she smiled. 'My brother, Ieuan, he speaks English – he is in the bydi.'

'Do your aunt and uncle speak English?' Xanthe asked anxiously.

'Uncle does.' Patience spread her shawl over the pine needles and sat down, sharing oatcakes and soft white cheese between them. 'And so – I think – does Motreb, but she learnt it from him. I've learnt what I know from listening to Mother and Father.'

'Why do you call your aunt "Motreb"?' Xanthe asked.

'It's Welsh for "aunt". When you write it down it's "modryb". I don't know why Uncle Huw has always been "uncle" and not "*ewythr*" – he just has. I'll teach you some words, if you like, so you can speak a bit by the time we arrive.'

'Yes please,' said Xanthe.

They munched in silence. The warm weather had come early and everything shimmered in the sun. The cheese had a pleasant, nutty flavour. Patience wondered if it was anything like the cheese her father had described making at Hafod. She wished he were with them. She wished she could tell him about the ride across the river. She wished very much that he wasn't dead.

'Aren't you going to finish your cheese?' enquired Xanthe.

'I've had enough.' Patience pushed it away. She looked at her friend's enquiring face. 'Xanthe,' she said hesitatingly, 'I've never asked – I've never liked to – but – what about your father? Where is he?'

Xanthe smiled wryly. 'I'd like to know that, too. And sometimes . . .' – she gave a half sigh 'sometimes I think I wouldn't like to know.'

'Oh, but why?' Patience sat up. 'Perhaps he could have helped you so that you wouldn't have had to run away when Rose Lea was taken over by the cruel planter.'

Xanthe was silent for a moment.

'I think,' she said quietly, looking at her hands, 'I think that my father *was* the cruel planter.'

Patience was speechless. She gazed at Xanthe in astonishment.

'Mother had told me,' Xanthe went on, 'that it didn't matter who my father was – that we were very lucky to have a good owner and to be together, and that was all that mattered.' She turned to Patience.

'Slaves often didn't live in families, anyway, you see. And even when they did, they were part of a much bigger group. It was different – quite different – from the lives of free people.' She clasped her arms around her knees. 'I'm not as dark-skinned as Mother was. That wasn't unusual either. The children of female slaves were often fathered by white overseers or by owners.'

'But,' Patience broke in, 'why do you think it was Francis Drummond? You're much too nice to have a father like that! How do you *know*?'

'I don't know,' Xanthe answered, 'not for certain, and I probably never will, but I've thought about it a lot. Francis Drummond sold Mother when she was fourteen – just before I was born. He got a good price for her because she was pregnant. And – have you ever noticed my toes?'

'Your toes? No – why?'

'My two big toes have no toenails. One of the stable-boys at Rose Lea had been a Drummond slave. He said Francis Drummond was born without any toenails.'

Patience frowned. She leant across and gave Xanthe a hug.

'Your mother was right,' she said. 'It doesn't matter! I'm sorry if I've made you sad.'

'You haven't.' Xanthe shook her head. 'I hardly ever think about it.' She lay back and looked up through the branches. 'And besides, now that we're far away from Liverpool, I don't feel at risk any more. No one could possibly harm me here – I feel quite safe. I think I shall enjoy living on a farm!' She closed her eyes.

Patience sat very still. Some of Xanthe's words had made her turn cold: 'He got a good price for her because she was pregnant.'

The matter-of-fact tone made it seem all the worse. The gulf between Xanthe's childhood and her own seemed so great. And yet here she was, lying beside her on the shawl, breathing the same air.

Patience looked about her. Everyone – herdsmen, dogs, Xanthe, even the flies – seemed to be having an afternoon nap, but she felt wide awake. She stood up and decided to explore.

8

The Stranger

Patience followed a stony path that skirted the farm wall. A cool breeze met her face as she rounded a corner and she saw that the farm lay on a ridge and that the track they were to follow wound steadily upward across higher, rougher ground. She surveyed the craggy, mountainous terrain. Her legs were still aching and she felt relieved that they were to ride from here on. Her ears caught the clink of harness and she followed the sound around the back of the stable and into the dark interior.

'Goot afternoon!' came a voice from the darkness.

'Good afternoon,' Patience replied, still blinded by sunlight.

'I am sattling your pony. You can tell me how high you want the stirrups.'

Gradually the face that owned the voice emerged out of the gloom. For a moment Patience thought that the farmer's wife had undergone a fairy transformation and become a man. But of course – this was Ieuan, the English-speaking brother! She crossed cautiously to the pony's side and stroked the soft neck. A bright eye glinted around at her. The matter of the stirrups was troublesome.

'I suppose we shall have to ride astride,' she pondered.

'You will – both of you – or you'll soon take a tumble. We haf no side saddle here and the cround is fery rough in parts.' Xanthe was two inches taller and Patience saw that she must sit in front if she wanted to see about her. Xanthe would therefore have her feet in the stirrups and be doing the 'proper' riding. She knit her brows.

'Of course,' Ieuan said, 'if you don't want to ride together, you can take it in turns.'

'I think,' Patience said, 'that we will ride together please – at least for today. Xanthe – my friend – will have to decide on the stirrup length then.'

'Ah yes – the dark young lady.' Ieuan bent to adjust the girth. 'A young man passed this way early this morning,' he remarked casually. 'He was asking about her.' It took a moment for his words to sink in.

'A young man! What sort of young man?'

'How many sorts are there?' Ieuan grinned and straightened up. 'An Enclishman. About twenty-two years of age, with a peard and a hat – out here.' He held out his hands to indicate a broad brim. Patience's thoughts immediately flew to the person she'd seen at the coaching inn at Liverpool – the young man who'd taken such an interest in Xanthe.

'Oh, and he had a pandage around his wrist,' Ieuan added. That confirmed it. Patience's mouth went dry. If only she'd mentioned him to Mr Morris at the time!

'He said he was looking for work,' Ieuan went on conversationally, leaning on the pony's rump, quite unaware of the impact of his words. 'Put I told him there was no work around here and to co north to the slate mines at Corwen – he'd stand a petter chance up there.'

'And did he go that way?' Patience's hands were clenched with tension.

'He tid. Put he said he would pe pack and that I was to let him know if your friend had passed py – and where she was going to.'

Patience's heart sank. She swallowed hard.

'Are you sure,' she asked, without very much hope, 'that it was Xanthe he sought?'

'A tark young laty in a creen ponnet accompanied by a fair young laty in a plue ponnet ant a minister of religion with them,' Ieuan quoted. 'How anyone could mistake William Gwyn for a minister of religion I can't say, put you two answer the description pretty well.'

'Did he say why he wanted to know?'

'He tid not. Only that he had urgent pusiness with the young laty. He offered me *money*!' – Ieuan uttered the word with contempt – 'put I am not to be pought!' He drew the reins over the pony's ears and prepared to lead her into the sunlight.

'Ieuan!' – Patience darted forward and gripped his arm. The intensity of her tone halted him and he gazed down in surprise at her flushed face. 'It's very important' – Patience tried hard to keep her voice level – 'that this person does not know where we are going! I'm sorry I cannot say more, but I fear very much that he means some harm to my friend. If he comes back, will you *promise* that you won't tell him you've seen us?'

'Means her some harm?' – Ieuan shook his head incredulously, his face a picture of concern. 'You neet not fear, miss. I am not in the hapit of tisclosing information to strangers!'

'Oh thank you!' cried Patience in relief. 'Oh and Ieuan – please don't tell anyone about this – not anyone!'

'I will not! – I will not!' Frowning, he led the little mare across the yard. Patience followed, her thoughts racing. If only Mr Morris were with her to give his advice! There could be no question of sharing the news with Xanthe, who was only now beginning to feel safe and who, in any case, could do nothing. Even Uncle Huw and Motreb, however sympathetic they might be to Xanthe's story, would have little understanding of the complex world of slavery and the skulduggery that surrounded it.

William Gwyn strode out of the farmhouse, followed by the farmer and his family.

'How do you like Peg?' the drover demanded, pointing at the pony. 'She's very docile – I've ridden her myself.'

'She's very nice,' Patience answered flatly. This

was to have been the high point of her journey – the moment she'd been looking forward to all day. But now she felt engulfed in a cloud of confusion and worry. Xanthe appeared at her side.

'Where did you go?' she asked, yawning. 'I thought you'd been spirited away.'

The sheep had been released and were already on their way. The business of mounting was supervised by Ieuan, who cupped his hands to form a mounting step. The girls were obliged to hitch up their skirts. Patience grasped the front of the saddle as Xanthe, behind her, was handed the reins.

'Haf a safe journey!' said Ieuan. 'You'll be at Maes Coch long before sunset.' He turned to Xanthe. 'Keep her on a firm rein to start off – she's a bit excited.' He patted Patience's hand. 'Ant ton't worry!'

'Don't worry about what?' Xanthe asked, as they moved off.

'About falling off, I suppose,' Patience lied.

'*Pob hwyl!*' shouted the farmer – 'All the best!'

'*Pob hwyl!*' echoed his relations, standing under the trees and waving. William Gwyn raised his hat. Xanthe turned Peg's head to follow the flock.

'I think this is going to be the best part of the journey,' she said happily, 'don't you?' Patience nodded absently as they began to climb the stony mountainside.

Peg stepped out. Her head bobbed rhythmically as the breeze lifted her mane. A moving pattern of sun and shadow turned the hills before them from blue to green and from green to gold. But they might have been riding across the sands of the desert, so firmly was Patience locked in her thoughts.

Who was this young man? What did he want? Whatever it was, he must want it a lot to offer Ieuan money when he had no work.

Mr Morris's words haunted her: 'Liverpool is full of rogues who could profit from Xanthe's illegal sale!' Surely this man couldn't be thinking of abducting her out here in the wilds – not on his own? But perhaps he wasn't on his own. Perhaps the story about looking for work was a decoy. Could there be others with him, hoping somehow to smuggle Xanthe back to Antigua to claim the reward? Or was it nothing to do with all that? She remembered Xanthe's anxious question: 'Do you think that I shall be wanted for murder?' Might this man be in the pay of some agent of the legal system or Captain Manders's family? Or did he intend to blackmail her in some way? It was all much too complex and confusing for Patience to be able to form any coherent ideas. She felt certain of only one thing: whatever this man's motives in pursuing Xanthe into Wales, there was precious little chance of their being well intentioned. Up until the time Patience had found her in the churchyard, everybody who'd had anything to do with Xanthe had wanted to exploit her in some way – Captain Manders,

Francis Drummond – even Mr Tresco. Everyone except the Reverend Clark, and he was at the bottom of the sea. Patience couldn't believe that this stranger could be harmless.

Her first thought when Ieuan had told her about him was that she must notify someone: as soon as they arrived at Hafod, she must write a letter explaining the situation and requesting help and reassurance. But when she considered it, even that notion began to evaporate. Who was there to write to? Mr Morris would be touring for a whole month or more, and to burden her mother with any more anxiety was unthinkable – in any case, how could she help? It was gradually becoming apparent that Patience was going to have to shoulder this new threat on her own – at least for the present.

She tried to recapture some of the carefree feeling of the morning, before they'd arrived at Bryn Glas, but a nagging anxiety was never far away. The terrain seemed to reflect her mood. Undulating hills had given way to high, dark crags and the track had narrowed, forcing the flock into a long, thin line between the outcrops. Often they were in shadow as the tall rocks obscured the sun, and Patience found herself periodically surveying the crags and ledges above them for anything that moved. William Gwyn's demeanour was the opposite of her own. A good lunch in the farmhouse, washed down by plenty of home-brewed ale, had put him in an uncharacteristically conversational mood, and in

Xanthe he found a captive audience. Riding alongside Peg he had embarked on a rambling narrative.

'. . . plenty of young women like yourselves – a bit older, perhaps. Farmers' daughters mostly, who want to earn some money – want to see the fashions as well. And some are on the lookout for husbands – there's not a very big choice for them up here in the hills.'

'And they walk with you all the way to London?' Xanthe sounded incredulous.

'All the way. They get work in the market gardens, you see, around Hammersmith way. That is why they call them *merched y gerddi* – the garden girls. Most come back with us at the end of the summer to bring their earnings home (we take beasts to the Smithfield market pretty regularly, you see). They are good girls for the most part, although a few go astray, of course, and end up as bad lots.'

Patience began to take an interest, curious to learn more about the bad lots. William Gwyn's voice rambled on and occasionally the herdsmen called to one another. Gradually the fears of the afternoon began to recede. After all, what harm could come to Xanthe in reality? Twelve herdsmen and the redoubtable drover were surely protection enough until they attained the safety of Hafod and Uncle Huw! Besides, if this young man spoke no Welsh, he'd be hard pressed to find anybody who could tell him where to find them!

The sun had sunk lower in the sky and the gnats had begun to bite. The thought of a square meal and a soft bed at Maes Coch was appealing. William Gwyn's solid form beside them was like a bulwark against the evening sky.

This time tomorrow, Patience thought, looking at a pale half-moon that showed itself above a sycamore tree, this time tomorrow, we'll be there. We'll have arrived at Hafod!

9

Journey's End

Two cats, a cockerel and a young sheepdog shot out of the open doorway of Hafod farm and took up guarded positions in the sunshine as a mighty crash and a scream resounded around the farmyard. In the kitchen, cavernous and dark, a red-faced Motreb Ann pushed her sleeves further up her rounded arms and swore – half in English and half in Welsh – at the iron cauldron that had dropped like a rock from its hook above the fire, dowsing the hearthstone with water.

'*Yr hen ddiawl!* You'll stay up there if it takes me all day!' From his cupboard bed in the corner, her husband, Huw, shook his head and gazed upwards in resignation.

'If you haven't got brawn, you have got to use brain!' he declared. He raised himself onto an elbow, wincing at the pain of his injured back, and pointed a long finger at the cauldron. 'Empty the water out, hook it up empty and fill it with a pitcher,' he instructed. 'You'll never lift it full!'

'But it will take me *all day* like that!' protested his wife. She passed a sleeve across her brow and glanced at the grandfather clock in the corner. 'And look, if William Gwyn is to time, the girls will he here in an hour and no hot water to wash after two days' travelling!'

Huw Penry sank back with a groan as she grasped the chains of the vessel anew.

'Please yourself!' he declared. 'But washing in cold water they'll be!'

'I'll help you, Mrs Penry!' A tall lad of about sixteen had appeared at the open doorway. Ducking under the lintel, he grasped the cauldron with strong hands and together they hooked it securely over the glowing peat.

'*Dyna fachgen da!*' – 'There's a good boy!' – Ann collapsed onto a stool and beamed up at the boy's good-humoured face. She rubbed her wrists. 'What would we do without you, Hywel Pugh?'

Hywel smiled.

'You won't have to do without me for a bit.' He took a broom and began sweeping the lake of spilt water out of the door. 'Things are pretty slack down at the forge, so Dad says I can come up here most days until Mr Penry's back on his feet.'

'I'll be back on my feet tonight!' came the voice from the corner. 'My niece is not having a cripple for an uncle!'

'Cripple you'll be if you get up too soon!' warned his wife. She rose and turned her attention to a crock of dough on the table. Plunging her arms into the mixture, she began pummelling it fiercely.

Outside, the little collie bitch crept from her hiding place behind a log pile and negotiated Hywel's broom. He gave her a reassuring pat.

'Good Fan!'

Huw had risen and was making painful progress to the doorway.

'If I'm to meet the young ladies, I'd best be off,' Hywel said. 'I shall be back in time to help Jenet with the milking, Mr Penry.'

'Take your time coming up the hill,' cautioned Ann, dipping her arms into a bucket of cold water and wiping off the sticky vestiges of dough. 'They are not used to hill walking.'

Hywel was already crossing the yard. 'Don't worry,' he called back. 'I'll tuck one under each arm!'

He vaulted the gate and was soon striding down the valley, swiping at the young bracken fronds with a switch, his copper hair glinting in the sun. Once across the brook at the valley bottom, he climbed up to the broad, green trackway and sat astride a stone wall.

Chewing on a long grass, he listened for the sound of the approaching drove.

Half a mile away Patience guided Peg along a downward track. It was her turn to take the reins and Xanthe, behind her, clasped her lightly around the waist. Both of them were dirty, hot and tired, but Patience felt buoyed up by the anticipation – half excited, half fearful – of arriving at her new home.

She wondered what her mother would have thought about the events of the previous night. There had been no soft bed, no hot meal, for typhoid had struck at Maes Coch and William Gwyn would allow no one into the house. A herdsman was despatched to Newtown for a doctor, riding through the night, and the girls had slept on sacks of hay under the stars, William Gwyn as sentinel beside them. The last of his bread and cheese had provided breakfast. Patience suspected that the itch on the back of her legs might be flea bites. She smiled to herself. In her sheltered Jamaica Street home, Florence had always insisted on bed – in a well-laundered nightgown – by eight o'clock, a thorough wash on rising, and a substantial breakfast to 'set her up for the day'. Perhaps now she was already installed in her new role at Culver Park? Patience wondered if her mother missed her and how long she would have to wait for a letter.

They were entering a broad valley, the drover showing no sign of his sleepless night. He pointed upward to where an eagle, with wings spread, seemed pinned like a badge to the sky.

'On the lookout for new lambs!' he remarked.

Patience scanned the landscape. Heather was giving way to gorse and gorse to bracken. This new, unknown land had been as familiar to her father as Jamaica Street had been to her. The drover was riding beside them. Perhaps he had known her father.

'Mr Gwyn' she hesitated. 'Have you known my uncle for long?'

'I have.'

'Then – you must have known my father, too?' A pause. The drover's face seemed more impassive than usual.

'I did.'

'So – did you know my mother, also, when she was young?'

Abruptly the drover urged his mount forward.

'Look where that pony of yours is going, young lady, or you'll end up in the gorse.' His voice was unusually gruff as he headed off a group of straying sheep and took up a position some distance ahead of the two girls. Mystified, Patience turned to look at Xanthe, who smiled and shook her head.

'You won't get any more out of him now,' she remarked. 'Perhaps your aunt . . .' Their speculation was interrupted by a shout from William Gwyn, who was standing in his stirrups and craning his neck.

'Journey's end ahead!' he called back to them. 'Your escort is waiting for you!'

Escort! Who could he mean? Startled, Patience crammed her bonnet onto her head and pulled on crumpled mittens. It seemed that their leisurely journey was to come to an abrupt end and she felt completely unprepared for the change. She fumbled to tie her bonnet strings, letting the reins fall slack. Butterflies fluttered in her stomach as, narrowing her eyes, she held up a hand against the sun.

'It's a young man,' Xanthe said. Beyond the bobbing backs of the sheep they could see a copper-headed youth laughing and exchanging mock insults with the herdsmen. He stood to attention as William Gwyn reined in beside him. The drover took Peg's reins from Patience's hands and drew them over the pony's head.

'Hywel Pugh, the blacksmith's son!' he announced. 'He will take you on to Hafod.' The girls slid to the ground and shook out their skirts as Hywel proffered a hand to each of them.

'How do you do,' said Patience. The boy grinned at the formality.

'You've had a long journey,' he said.

'You speak English!' Xanthe exclaimed in relief.

'All blacksmiths speak English,' Hywel replied. 'They have to – the forge is the place where travellers ask the way.' His broad face, freckled like Patience's own, was open and friendly and he had an air of cheerful confidence. Patience decided that she liked him. She turned to bid farewell to William Gwyn and to thank him – she'd prepared a little speech in her head.

'Oh!' she cried, disconcerted. 'He's gone!' The drover's broad back was already receding as he rode after the flock, leading Peg, riderless, beside him.

'Goodbye, Mr Gwyn!' Patience called out, 'and thank you!'

Without turning his head, the drover raised his stick in salute as his mount plodded on.

'He could have said goodbye!' said Patience, frowning.

'He's like that,' Hywel told her, leading the way to a gap in the wall and entering a rough meadow. 'He can't bear fuss or ceremony. But he's a good old sort – you just have to take him as you find him.'

Evidently, Patience thought, still feeling slightly affronted at the drover's abrupt departure. The girls picked their way between thistles and cowpats.

'How is my uncle?' Patience enquired.

'Better, but he can't do much yet. He was climbing into the hayloft when he missed his footing and fell – it must have been a good twelve feet. But he's a tough man – he'll be fit in time for the shearing in July. It's a bad time to be laid up, though, with the first of the hay coming ready. That's why I'm here,' Hywel went on, 'to lend a hand till he's better. It makes a change from shoeing beasts. A forge can be a pretty warm place to work in.'

'You must see quite a lot of comings and goings,' Patience observed.

'There's not much going on we don't know about,' Hywel agreed, smiling.

'Are there any strangers in the area at the moment – people you don't know?' Hywel looked at her curiously.

'No more than usual, I'd say. Two new young ladies at Hafod is news enough – your uncle had a record number of offers of help with getting the hay in!'

Xanthe laughed. Patience was unsure what to make of the remark. A large workforce would certainly make it feel a lot safer. But if their arrival was the talk of the district . . .

A row of stepping stones crossed the stream, each one a jump away from the next. The girls followed Hywel cautiously.

Patience stopped and looked down at the rounded pebbles that formed the bed. Suddenly she recalled her father describing how he and Huw had been paid a farthing a sackful by their father to carry stones from the stream to cobble the muddy farmyard and how, between them they'd earned sixpence. Enough to guess the weight of an ox at Abercroes fair and to buy apples dipped in sugar to eat on the long, moonlit walk home. She stared through the eddying water.

'Need a hand?' Hywel called. She jumped the last few stones and followed the others up the hill through the first of the cow parsley. The ground rose steeply and they climbed without speaking, the late afternoon sun warm on their backs.

'Is it far?' Patience was out of breath. Hywel shook his head. He stopped beside a stunted oak-tree and waited for the girls to catch up.

'You're not used to country life, then?'

'No,' said Patience.

'Yes,' said Xanthe, simultaneously.

'Xanthe lived in the country when she was younger,' Patience said. 'And now . . . she's taking a holiday with me.' Hywel nodded slowly, looking from one to the other. Patience, self-conscious under his frank gaze, was relieved when the climb was over.

Hywel helped each of them up the last, steep slope and onto a flat, grassy path that ran at right angles to their climb and parallel with the droveway on the opposite side of the valley. He turned right along the path and pointed ahead.

'Hafod,' he said, 'is just beyond that far bend.'

It was good to be on level ground.

'What lies behind us?' Xanthe asked, as they made their way along the track.

'Old slate workings,' Hywel told her, 'abandoned this long time. Not a good place to go.'

'Oh, why?' Patience was interested.

'It's a grim old spot. And dangerous. The last person to go there was a shepherd looking for a lost ewe. He's never been found.'

Patience looked over her shoulder and was about to ask more when Xanthe said, 'I can see smoke.'

Apprehension gripped Patience's stomach. What if her aunt and uncle didn't like her? What if she didn't like them? What if it was all going to be a dreadful mistake?

Hywel pushed open a wide gate across the roadway, holding back a heavy branch of elder that hung over it, brushing their bonnets with creamy pollen.

And there it was. A long, low, red-washed dwelling, built of massive, boulder-like stones, its thatched roof shelving steeply up to two, squat chimneys, one of them smoking vigorously. For Patience, the scent of elderflower was to be forever linked with that first, almost fearful, sight of Hafod.

She linked arms with Xanthe, as much for reassurance as to help negotiate the hard ridges of dried mud at the entrance to the yard. Everything was still and very quiet. Then Hywel let fall the latch of the gate behind them and the sound caused the house, the yard, the byre and the fields behind it to erupt into sudden, tumultuous life.

10

Hafod

Patience often looked back to that moment when all that was to become so familiar had appeared so alien and when the people whom she was to regard as her family had seemed for a while like strangers. The images of her first five minutes at Hafod were to remain as sharp and as clear as magic lantern pictures and yet the sounds that had made up the general clamour seemed, in recollection, to have been strangely interchangeable. She could never be quite sure whether the cries of delight had come from her aunt, as she darted from the open doorway, apron flying, or from the gander who'd glided before her with outstretched wings, nor which of them had been doing the squawking. Fan, of course had been responsible for the barking before she'd flattened her stomach on the ground and flapped her feather of a tail at Xanthe's proffered glove. And a herd of stocky black cows had chosen that moment to come down from their rough, hillside pasture for milking, as they had done at ten past six every evening of their lives, following their route to the very cobblestone. Two young women in silk bonnets standing in their path had caused them to deviate not an inch, but to Patience and Xanthe it appeared that they had been targeted for mass assault and each, in a vain attempt to hide behind the other, had very quickly become giddy. Hywel, shouting and prodding at the animals, had been joined by Gwilym, the toothless farmhand, who had emerged, grinning, from behind a hayrick to add his deep voice to the chorus and persuade the animals to change course. The only silent onlookers had been pretty, deaf and dumb Jenet Gwen, who'd peeped shyly from the doorway of the dairy before disappearing abruptly inside – and Uncle Huw.

Now, as Xanthe and Patience emerged, gasping from Motreb's powerful hugs, they saw that Uncle Huw was leaning against the doorframe of the farmhouse, the corners of his mouth turning down in a wry smile, as he looked on. Patience had been afraid that he might resemble her father and that she'd find it hard to look him in the face. She was relieved to see that there was little to show they had been brothers. Where her father had been squarely built and broad-faced, with black, curly hair, Uncle Huw was tall and spare with fine, narrow features. The hands he held out in greeting were long and slender – more like those of an artist than of a hard-working hill-farmer.

'You've taken your time,' he teased them dryly. 'We were expecting you for breakfast!'

'*Paid a'u poeni nhw!*' Motreb remonstrated – 'Don't tease. They are here safe and sound!'

Motreb Ann was very short and everything about her – eyes, face, arms, in fact her entire person – was completely round. Patience had never before met a grown-up the same height as herself whom she was able to look directly in the eye. She rather liked the experience and smiled happily into her aunt's glowing face.

Blinded from the sunlight, the girls were led into the blackness of the kitchen, their only point of reference a row of pewter plates glinting dimly on the dresser. Wonderful smells assailed them – fresh bread, smoking peat, straw, chicken meal and dried herbs, of which Patience recognised only the bread.

The room had scarcely begun to take shape before Motreb steered them into the *parlwr*, brightly lit by a square window. It had horsehair chairs and a faded print of the king and queen above the empty fireplace. Patience privately decided that she liked the kitchen best. But here, on the table, stood a large and steaming china bowl of water, folded towels and a dish of little, round balls of soap scented with lavender. Patience was soon to discover that soap, like everything else at Hafod, was home-made by Motreb and Jenet Gwen.

As the two girls soaked their hands in the fragrant water and pressed warm squares of flannel to their sunburnt faces, Motreb hurried in and out with more jugs, more towels and two pairs of a curious kind of

94

footwear which she called 'pattens' to replace their muddy boots. They resembled leather sandals with wooden soles nearly two inches high. Motreb wore some herself, and they clattered noisily on the stone-flagged floor.

'Come and eat when you are clean,' she instructed, carrying their boots into the kitchen and closing the door behind her.

The little room was cool and silent. They looked at one another.

'Here at last!' said Patience.

'And safe,' said Xanthe. She lifted the bowl onto the floor and they sat on the horsehair sofa, blissfully soaking their feet, as the king and queen looked on.

They were never to see the lavender soap again, nor the china bowl. They were wrapped in linen and stored away for the next visitor. From then on, it was to be cold water from the well and large blocks of hard, yellow soap.

The pattens felt strange. The girls clacked awkwardly into the kitchen and were put to sit at a three-legged table near the door. 'Eat all you can!' Motreb commanded and they were happy to obey. Ham, preserves, newly-baked bread and fresh butter were dispatched as rapidly as politeness would allow. Motreb Ann made conversation unnecessary by providing a lively monologue as she refilled their plates and topped up their cups with strong, dark tea, scooped into the pot from a locked wooden box – a rare treat. Welsh words were inserted without pause when English ones escaped her, so there was no interruption to the flow: they couldn't imagine how much she'd been looking forward to their arrival – two ready-made daughters of her very own! And what bonnets! They would have to tell her about the fashions, so that she and Jenet could keep up. But there! They would surely find it dull out here after all the excitement of city life!

Patience glanced at Xanthe, reflecting that some of the excitement had been quite dispensable.

The home-cured ham was delicious.

'No more cheese!' whispered Xanthe thankfully.

'Cheese!' exclaimed Motreb, making for the cupboard, 'you can have all the cheese you want!'

'No thank you,' the girls chorused hastily, and Motreb, returning to her seat beside them, resumed her discourse: their arrival was the talk of the district, of course (Patience frowned) – John Penry's daughter and her friend coming back to Hafod! Not that she took after her father one bit – just as well, with his large hands and square shoulders. So tragic, her mother being widowed suddenly like that! They still couldn't really believe it. But there it was – the Lord knew best, she supposed.

Patience looked at her aunt. The words of sympathy were at odds with her abstracted manner and Patience realised that Motreb Ann had probably never known her father very well. Uncle Huw smiled quietly across to her from his corner by the fire.

Suddenly a shadow blocked the light from the doorway and Hywel stepped inside.

'Making up for lost time I see!' – he nodded at the laden table. Patience thought him familiar and looked away.

'Milking all done, Mrs Penry!' he continued cheerfully. 'Milk in the dairy, cows back on the hill. I'll be up in the morning. *Nos da*, all!'

'*Nos da!*' they all chorused.

Motreb rose reluctantly to join Jenet in the dairy and Xanthe began to gather up the dishes, but Huw raised his hand.

'Off duty tonight – you can start to do your share in the morning!'

Xanthe smiled and obediently sat down again.

'How far are you able to walk?' she asked.

'As far as the end of the yard – if I have a young lady to help me!'

He placed a hand on Xanthe's shoulder and the three made careful progress out into the cool, evening air. Patience glanced enviously into the open door of the dairy. Before long she might even take her very own butter to market, as her grandmother and great grandmother had done in those funny, tall hats she'd seen in pictures.

Huw gestured towards a stone wall next to a gate, exactly opposite the one they'd entered by. They leant their elbows on the flat stones. Small fields fell steeply away towards the valley bottom and behind them the rough hillside rose up to a stony crag, clumps of gorse and heather glowing in the dusk.

'From here,' said Huw, 'you can see the whole of the farm.' He made a broad sweep with his arm. Choosing his words with the care of one speaking a foreign language, he explained that they were yeoman farmers. This meant that the farm belonged to him, as it had to his forebears. He paid no rent, as most of the neighbouring tenant farmers did, but there were still taxes and tithes. Prices had dropped in the markets and times had been hard of late – much harder than when his father had been alive and when brother John had been with them.

'Then,' said Huw, 'we were three strong pairs of hands and the work of the farm got done – like that!' – he snapped his fingers. 'But now there is only me and Gwilym, the hired man. Ann and Jenet often have to do the work of men as well as dairying and the women's work.' He turned his back on the fields and leant against the wall as Motreb Ann and Jenet came out of the dairy to join them. 'So you see,' he smiled ruefully, 'there aren't many minutes of the day going begging.'

'I shall be able to help,' Xanthe ventured. 'I can make cheese – and butter.' Motreb flung up her arms and gave a cry of delight. 'An angel has been sent from heaven!' she exclaimed, 'to our very doorstep!' Then she frowned. 'But how did you learn to do that in Liverpool? Surely Florence doesn't have room for a cow?' Xanthe and Patience looked at one another and Patience realised that she had never asked her mother just how much Motreb and Uncle Huw had been told about Xanthe. Not, it seemed, a great deal.

'Xanthe lived in the West Indies before she came to us,' she explained. 'Mother and the Reverend Morris thought she'd be safe here in Wales – that's why she came with me.'

'Safe from what?' – Motreb's eyes were rounder than usual.

Patience turned to Xanthe.

'Will you explain? I think they need to know.'

Xanthe nodded and looked enquiringly at Huw.

'Then the sooner we are all sitting around the fire the better,' he declared. The sun had set and a sharp breeze blew off the hillside as they re-entered the kitchen.

Jenet darted forward to seize a leather bellows almost as large as herself from beside the chimney. Thrusting the nozzle into the fire, she pumped away vigorously and the dim glowing peat erupted into a blaze that lit the darkened room. The two girls settled down on two high-backed seats that faced each other on either side of the hearth.

As Xanthe's story unfolded, Jenet Gwen sat motionless. Hearing nothing, she watched the movements of Xanthe's lips, occasionally glancing quickly at the others to gauge their reactions. Patience wondered how much she could understand. She had one of the prettiest faces Patience had ever seen – small and pink with deep brown eyes and perfect pearly teeth.

Her glossy black hair was gathered at the nape of her neck. Patience sighed, remembering her own freckles and wispy locks. She tried to decide whether being deaf was a price worth paying for being beautiful and concluded that, as she was neither, there was no way of finding out.

She glanced around the faces lit by the fire. Xanthe had got to the part where she had seen Patience sitting on the tombstone. Huw was leaning forward and Motreb's hand was clasped across her mouth. Xanthe herself seemed to have developed a kind of immunity to the sadness of her tale. Perhaps she had relived it so often that it had lost some of its impact, or that talking about her mother had made her seem a little less far away. When she had finished, Huw placed a hand on Xanthe's shoulder.

'This is your home as much as it is Patience's,' he told her. 'You are safe with us.' Xanthe smiled at him and they all sat in silence for a moment, the grandfather clock ticking quietly. Patience wondered if she should mention the stranger. In the warmth and security of her new home the idea that he could pose any kind of threat seemed ludicrous. She opened her mouth to speak, but Motreb gave a loud yawn and Huw stood up.

'Time for bed!' he announced. 'The reapers will be here tomorrow to help us bring in the hay.' He turned and opened a cylindrical box nailed to the chimney breast and drew out a handful of tapers. Holding their wicks in the fire, he waited for them to ignite with their own, pale flames then handed them carefully to his wife, who secured them in a pincer-like holder. She led the way up the broad staircase, Jenet Gwen following.

The tapers' light was faint, but the girls could see that the stairs gave onto a square space that was part landing, part bedroom and part store. A makeshift bed took up some of the floor and strings of onions hung along the walls.

'Jenet Gwen sleeps here,' Motreb explained, 'because Huw is in her bed in the kitchen since his injury. I sleep in there,' she gestured to a door on the right, 'and you are in here.' She led the way through a door to the left. Patience turned to mouth '*Nos da*' to Jenet before following.

Two starched nightdresses were laid out on the double bed, which took up most of the room, apart from a chest and some round bales of unspun wool, which gave off an oily, pungent smell.

Motreb placed the tapers carefully on the chest.

'Make sure you blow them out well.' She pointed upwards. 'The roof is straw thatch, remember.' She planted a final kiss on each of their cheeks and turned to leave.

'Motreb,' said Patience, sitting on the edge of the bed, 'how old is Jenet Gwen?'

Motreb pursed her lips. 'She must be all of sixteen now, I would think. It's surely seven years since Huw brought her back here.'

'Back from where?'

'Why back from the hiring fair at Pont Bethel. I can see her now, shivering in the corner of the cart, a little, skinny thing. We didn't have any use for a nine-year-old, of course, let alone one that couldn't speak or hear a word, but Huw said he couldn't have left her in the market place, with the men all leering and passing remarks and her not understanding a thing, poor little soul. She's been with us ever since. A good little worker, remember, and like a daughter to me.'

'But where had she come from?' Patience persisted.

'There's a girl you are for questions! Look, the tapers will be burnt out, and you still dressed! All we can say is that she was found by a herdsman over Ffestiniog way in a poor *bwthyn bach*, her family all dead of the typhoid and her the only survivor. And we only found that out three years back. There now – into bed, the pair of you!' And Motreb whisked out of the door.

'What's a *bwthyn bach*?' Xanthe asked, unrolling her stockings.

'A tiny cottage where poor people live,' Patience said, 'like some of the ones we passed on the way.' She clambered into the bed in a nightdress big enough to hold two of her, the straw mattress rustling beneath her. Xanthe blew the tapers out and wet the wicks so they sizzled.

Lying in the darkness, they listened to the silence. Occasionally the thatch creaked above them. Now that the tension and excitement of the journey was over and Hafod had become a reality, Patience was conscious of a feeling of bleakness. They were here to stay – there was no going back. Far away an unknown dog barked into the night. For the first time since the mail coach had carried them out of Liverpool, Patience felt homesick for Jamaica Street with its oil lamps and brocade curtains and the comforting smell of mothballs and fried onions. She reached out to touch Xanthe's back and buried her face in the pillow.

11

Pigs, Pitchforks and a Pony

It was mid morning before Patience awoke from the deepest sleep of her life. She stared uncomprehendingly at the underside of the steep thatch as her mind struggled to catch up with the events of the previous day. The whole room was flooded with light from a window near the floor. It was strange to be in a bedroom that had no ceiling, no curtains and no wallpaper. The rough stones of the walls and the wide, oaken floorboards looked so old that they might have grown directly out of the hillside, as indeed they once had.

Patience tried to work out how the house was arranged. She knew that the kitchen had no rooms above it and that the gallery that ran along its far end formed the landing where Jenet Gwen slept. So Motreb and Uncle Huw's bedroom must lie over the parlour and this room – must be directly over the dairy! Patience felt a sense of achievement at having worked it all out.

The yearning for Jamaica Street had faded with the night. This, after all, had been Father's home – the place where he'd played and grown up. She'd try to make it her home, too, and learn all the things a farmer's niece ought to know.

It wasn't until she sat up that Patience noticed Xanthe wasn't there. Puzzled, she slid off the bed and knelt to look out of the window. Sharp-edged shadows lay across the yard and a cockerel with raised foot stood motionless by the barn door. His coloured feathers became brilliant as he strutted into the sunshine. Suddenly, Xanthe appeared from the cowshed next to the barn. She was wearing a pink, cotton sunbonnet and carrying two wooden pails full of milk suspended from a yoke across her shoulders. She walked carefully, head bent, but with an air that was confident and purposeful as she disappeared into the dairy immediately below.

Patience stood up. She was gripped with a sensation so strong and so totally unexpected that she had to reach for the bedpost to steady herself. She felt overwhelmed with a desire to sink Xanthe's serene face into the milk pail. She dropped onto the bed, bewildered by a feeling that was powerful, new and horrible. This was *her* farm, *her* dairy, *her* special inheritance! And now the role she had been imagining for herself the whole of the long journey here had been taken over by someone else – someone she was supposed to be rescuing! A small voice at the back of her head told her that she was being unfair and ridiculous, but the voice did nothing to counter the cold, grey jealousy that lay across her chest. Below, she could hear the clatter of

dairy utensils and Xanthe's voice mingling with
Motreb Ann's. Struggling to dress, Patience forced
herself into what she knew her mother would regard
as a 'proper' frame of mind: Xanthe had nothing and
nobody. How could Patience begrudge her the
satisfaction of contributing some of her skills to her
new life? After all, there were more than enough
tasks for both of them, as Uncle Huw had made clear.

Feeling a little more in control, she looked around
for a mirror, but there was none. Using her fingers as
a makeshift comb, she tied her hair back with a
ribbon and bent to fasten the unfamiliar pattens. As
she did so, Xanthe emerged again into the yard and
looked up at the window. Seeing Patience, her face
broke into a smile of such openness and pleasure
that Patience felt ashamed. She smiled weakly back
and turned to unlatch the bedroom door.

The kitchen seemed deserted, but as Patience
reached the bottom of the stairs, she noticed Gwilym
rinsing his hands in a bucket by the door. Shaking
them dry, he ran a hand over his scrubby beard and
grinned at her.

'I've been feeding the pigs,' he said in Welsh. His
voice was deep and his words strangely muffled – a
consequence of a mouth devoid of teeth. Patience
felt pleased she could understand.

'How many are there?' The farmhand sat down on
a stool, mouthing the numbers to himself.

'Twelf!' he announced triumphantly, reverting to
English. Patience smiled and poured some milk from

a pitcher on the table into a small bowl, as she had seen Uncle Huw doing. She sat on the bottom stair to drink it.

'What will happen to them – the baby pigs?'

'They will be fattened up over the summer.' Gwilym told her. 'Some will go to market, and then in November the rest will be –' he passed a finger across his throat, 'slottered! Food for the winter!' He pointed to one of the rafters, where a side of bacon, wrapped in muslin, hung from a hook. 'That,' he explained, 'was the grandmother of these piglets.'

'I see.' Patience placed her empty bowl back on the table and considered the matter. If this process was to be a regular feature of the farming year, she needed to be prepared for it.

'Who does the slaughtering exactly, and where does it take place?'

'*Fi sy'n gneud e* – I do it. And Huw Penry and sometimes Llew Nant-y-Coed. We take the animals to a pen below the well, so there is plenty of water to wash away the blood – the stream runs red. Everyone knows when it's pig-sticking at Hafod – they can hear the beasts screaming!' He beamed amiably across at Patience, who sat down suddenly on a stool. She decided to change the subject quickly in case he elaborated further.

'What did you do, Gwilym, before you came to Hafod?'

'Worked in the slate mine up the hill.' He jerked his head to the right. 'Very hard work, but good pay.

It closed down years back – not enough labour to be had. There's tunnels and caverns there you could lose a hundred head of cattle in – some say it is haunted.'

Ghosts or not, Patience instantly determined to make the mine her hideaway when the pigs were to be killed. She felt relieved that a ready-made retreat lay close at hand. Gwilym rose and made for the door. He had a curious slouching gait.

'Your aunt has been asking for you – she's in the dairy.'

Left alone, Patience contemplated the second unwelcome shock of the morning. Farming wasn't going to be all milking cows and making hay. She wiped her milky upper lip with the back of her hand, and followed the sound of voices into the dairy.

'There you are!' Motreb beamed at her. The room was whitewashed and cool. Patience closed the door behind her, shutting out images of blood and screaming pigs.

'I'm skimming cream off ready to make butter,' Xanthe told her from behind a long, slate trough full of creamy milk. 'You can do the last bit.' She held out a wooden disc and showed Patience how to pass it over the surface of the milk. Patience concentrated, tilting the skimmer so that only the cream was gathered up. The task was satisfying and soothing.

'Two new dairymaids!' Motreb clucked. 'I can retire to be a lady!'

She untied her apron and hung it on a peg. 'I'm

going down to join the reapers in the hayfield. Come after me with those.' She pointed to four pitchers of buttermilk lined up against the wall and hurried out into the sunshine.

'Now,' Xanthe said, 'we must scoop the skimmed milk back into the buckets for the calves.'

'How do you *know*?' Patience asked, joining in the task, but unable to conceal her irritation at Xanthe's confident management of affairs.

'Your aunt told me. And in any case, it's exactly what we used to do at Rose Lea.'

'Was the dairy there like this one?'

'A little, but much, much bigger. It had blue and white tiles and a high arched roof.' They worked in silence until Xanthe said, 'Oh, Patience – I found this!' She picked up a round, wooden butter stamp, carved with an oak leaf and 'H' for Hafod. Patience took it from her. 'Turn it over,' Xanthe said. The underside had a neat little handle and the letters 'JP'.

'Father made it!' Patience exclaimed, running her fingers around the pattern. She held the smooth wood to her cheek.

'I'm sorry I was cross,' she told Xanthe, as they covered the pails with a cloth.

'You weren't *very* cross!' Xanthe laughed. She handed over two of the pitchers and propped the door open with her back for Patience to pass out. They crossed the yard, looking for the path to the hayfield and found it winding around the corner of the house.

All the windows of Hafod faced the farmyard, as if the house had decided to turn its back on the valley and the haymakers, now toiling in rows the length of the steep fields. The pitchers became heavy and buttermilk splashed on their toes. They put them down to rest their arms. Patience shaded her eyes. Below them the scythes glinted rhythmically. In a neighbouring field bonneted women wielded long pitchforks to toss the hay. It was very hot. Jenet Gwen dropped her fork and waved both arms as they advanced down the path.

In the shade of a rowan Motreb was spreading out a cloth. She instructed the girls to spoon oatmeal into bowls and add a generous helping of buttermilk. The haymakers began to gather round, mopping their damp faces and casting curious glances at Xanthe's unfamiliar, dark face.

In the hum of talk, Patience repeatedly heard herself referred to as '*merch* John Penry'. She blushed as she and Xanthe became the focus of so many pairs of eyes. It was a relief when they could carry their bowls to a far corner of the field where Uncle Huw sat with his back against a dry stone wall. He raised a crutch in greeting. Motreb and Jenet joined them on the grass.

'Bwyd gwaith nawr,' Motreb said. 'Working food now – ham and eggs tonight!' Patience tried not to think too much about the ham. The oatmeal tasted like a slightly sour version of porridge and they ate in silence for a while, Huw occasionally calling out to one of the resting haymakers. Patience relaxed for the first time. They were beginning to feel like a family.

Huw was busying himself winding cord around the shaft of a rake that showed signs of splitting. He caught Patience's eye.

'We have to look after our tools now,' he said. 'There's not been a decent carpenter in the village since your father went away.'

Patience looked puzzled.

'But I thought Father went to Liverpool because there was no work here.'

Huw raised his eyebrows. 'Is that what he told you?'

Patience nodded. 'Isn't it true?'

Huw looked at Motreb and Patience looked at both of them.

'Will you tell her?' Huw asked.

'No, indeed, not I!' his wife replied. 'She's your niece – you tell her!'

'Oh, please *one* of you tell me!' Patience pleaded, looking from one to the other. Her aunt was pointedly busying herself with the tablecloth. Huw sighed and smiled wryly at his niece.

'Your mother was a handsome woman,' he remarked.

'She still is,' Patience said, wondering where this was leading. She seated herself directly in front of her uncle, forcing him to continue.

'But . . .' Huw hesitated, 'her father was not a

wealthy man. Highly respected, remember, but no money to mention and with nothing to leave Florence after his day. His best chance of providing for her was to find a husband with, so to speak, something behind him.'

Xanthe edged nearer to listen.

'Well, like I said, she was a good-looking lass and very refined. Our John was mad about her. She was all he talked about, and I think she gave him a good bit of encouragement!' Patience giggled. 'The trouble was,' Huw went on, 'John had a rival. And Florence's father favoured the rival because it was rumoured that one day he'd be a wealthy man.' Huw shifted his weight, wincing slightly. Motreb had rejoined them and sat watching Huw's face and nodding now and then. 'I'll never forget the day,' Huw said, 'that John came up the track from the village, his face white as ash. "It's all over," he said. "Florence Jones is engaged to be married!" He didn't speak to us for the rest of the day. Next morning there was a note on the kitchen table: he'd gone to look for work in Liverpool and taken Florence with him.'

'They eloped!' cried Patience, kneeling upright and clasping her hands. 'Oh – how *romantic*!'

Hugh smiled grimly. 'And romance was all they had to put in their stomachs for quite a while. Florence's father took it badly – he died within the year. By the time you came along, John had found employment, of course. And he wrote home regularly, I'll give him that, but no doubt he felt a bit guilty at leaving his old father. Could be the reason he didn't tell you about it all.'

'I'm sure he meant to,' Patience said loyally. 'I'm sure he would have done eventually. But – what happened to the rival? Did he become a wealthy man?'

Huw and Motreb laughed. 'He did indeed,' Huw said, 'although you may not think so to look at him. He brought you both here yesterday!'

Xanthe and Patience looked at one another open-mouthed.

'Oh!' Patience cried. 'Oh, poor William Gwyn!

'Poor!' exclaimed her aunt, tossing back a lock of hair, 'poor indeed! William Gwyn is the wealthiest man in North Wales! Nobody knows how much money he's made out of cattle-dealing over the years, but it's rumoured that he owns a big house in London and that even Sir Emrys Evans of Tŷ Mawr – the MP – owes him money!'

'Then why in the world,' asked Xanthe, 'does he still work as a drover?'

Huw shook his head. 'A lot of people have wondered that. I think he simply loves the life. It's all he's ever known. He's a good man – honest as the day, but there's a lot more to him than meets the eye. He's a dark horse!'

He reached for his crutch and Motreb helped him to his feet.

'Well, now – there's food for thought for you,

young lady!' she declared, as she and Huw made towards the path. 'Sit in the sun for a while, the pair of you!' she called over her shoulder. 'there'll be work enough later on, preparing harvest supper for all of these!' – she waved a hand towards the toiling reapers.

The girls watched them make their way up the hill.

'No wonder the harvesters were taking such an interest in you!' Xanthe said, sucking on a straw.

Patience lay back and gazed up at the blue sky. She remembered the intense way William Gwyn would sometimes gaze into her face when he thought she wasn't looking. She wondered if he'd loved her mother very much, and how her mother would have felt when she learnt who was to conduct them to Hafod.

'What would it have been like having William Gwyn for a father instead of mine?' she mused.

Xanthe laughed. 'Well, then you wouldn't be you – you'd be somebody else!'

Gradually the hum of flies blended with the voices of the haymakers and Patience fell asleep. In her dream it was winter and snowflakes were falling on her upturned face. She tried to brush them off and heard someone laughing. She opened her eyes. The sun had gone behind a cloud and someone was flicking grass seed at her. She turned her head and, squinting in the brightness, she saw Hywel crouching a few feet away, grinning wickedly. Patience sat up abruptly, checking to see that her skirt was decently arranged.

'What time is it?' she demanded, confused, 'And where did you come from?'

'It's about four o'clock,' Hywel replied in his slow, unruffled voice, 'and I've just brought your uncle's hay wain up from the forge. My dad's been mending a wheel on it and – it had your trunk on board! The carter brought it over from Ruthin this morning.'

'Our trunk!' Patience scrambled to her feet. 'Does Xanthe know?'

Hywel nodded.

'But she won't open it till you're there. Jenet is waiting to see all your smart clothes. It felt as though you had enough to clothe all the girls in Denbighshire!'

They began to climb the hill.

'It's not all clothes,' Patience said, struggling to keep up. 'There are books – and a sewing box – and presents for Motreb and . . .' but Hywel was already around the bend.

The trunk stood on the cobbles. The sight of the battered leather was welcoming and Patience hurried to unclasp the catch. As she raised the lid, Woolly Mary's button eyes gazed out and Patience slammed it shut, hoping Hywel hadn't noticed. 'We'll unpack later,' she declared, as Xanthe emerged from the kitchen.

'Hywel brought a letter for your aunt and uncle,'

she said. 'They seem a bit flustered – at least your aunt does.'

In the kitchen Huw and Motreb were conversing rapidly in Welsh.

'Have you heard of the Reverend Elijah Tonks?' Motreb demanded abruptly of her niece. Patience confessed that she had not. Distractedly, her aunt fanned herself with a plate.

'He's a very eminent preacher,' Huw explained. 'An evangelist. He draws hundreds to hear him speak. He's on a grand tour of Wales and is coming to preach at our chapel in July. The deacons want him to stay here, at Hafod. It's a great honour, of course, but a bit of a shock to your aunt. I suppose we shall have to agree.' His tone was less than enthusiastic. Motreb was pacing up and down distractedly, muttering about best sheets and putting up a bed in the parlour.

'If it's not until July,' Xanthe said, 'there'll be plenty of time to prepare for him – and we'll all help.'

Ann sat down, reassured by Xanthe's calm words.

'We've not entertained an important man from the chapel before,' she explained apologetically. 'But I daresay he eats and sleeps, much the same as you and me!'

'Yes, indeed!' her husband agreed. 'And has to pay his bills. And suffers with corns and indigestion!'

Ann looked shocked. 'Indigestion? A minister of religion?'

In the midst of the laughter, Hywel's head appeared around the door.

'I'm taking our horse back down to the forge, Mr Penry. Dad says you can settle for the wagon wheel when he sees you.' Patience looked out into the yard. A neat, black cob was tethered to the gatepost. It seemed to be gazing straight at her.

'Are you riding down?' she asked Hywel.

He nodded. 'Want to come?' Patience looked at her aunt.

'Go, if you want to,' Motreb said. 'You'll be safe enough with Hywel. Xanthe, too, if she wants to.'

But Xanthe shook her head. 'I'm not as keen on riding as Patience is. Besides, I'd like to carry on with the butter-making before the harvesters are here.'

Patience was already beside the horse, stroking its neck.

'What's her name?'

'It's a "he",' Hywel said. 'He's called Diamwnt – Diamond.' He helped Patience onto Diamond's bare back and sprang up behind her.

'Supper at seven o'clock, remember!' Motreb called, as they clopped out through the gate, Patience holding onto a handful of mane, Hywel's arm firmly around her waist. Diamond was taller than Peg had been and the ground seemed a long way down. Fan loped along beside them. Trotting without a saddle was uncomfortable and Hywel guided Diamond off the track and onto the turf.

'We'll take a short cut,' he announced. 'Hold on tight!' He gave the horse's sides a brisk kick and Patience caught her breath as Diamond broke into a canter, which rapidly became a gallop. The air rushed past her face. Grass, trees and bushes became a blur as Diamond's hooves thundered over the rough ground. Half terrified and half excited, Patience clung to the flying mane as they cleared gorse bushes and rocks, sometimes splashing over boggy peat, sometimes pounding across firm turf with Fan a white streak beside them. A hazel hedge loomed up and Patience felt herself slipping.

'I'm falling!' she cried, but Hywel tightened his grasp and urged Diamond on. With neck extended, the horse leapt the hedge, tucking his forelegs beneath him. They landed with a clatter onto the road, pulling up breathlessly before the open doorway of the forge. Hywel jumped down, and Patience, with shaking knees, slithered unsteadily to the ground. Her skirt was torn, her hair awry and her pink face streaked with mud. She smiled triumphantly up at Hywel.

'Remember,' he told her gravely, 'we rode down the track – very sedately!'

Patience scarcely had the breath to laugh and bent to stroke the heaving sides of little Fan, who pressed against her leg.

'Galloping again!' said a deep voice behind her. 'My son has been leading you astray, Miss Penry!'

She turned to see the smiling face of Hywel's

father. 'But there, I was just as bad at his age – worse if anything! How are you liking it at Hafod?'

Patience had just recovered the power of speech. 'Very much – and thank you for sending our trunk up.'

The blacksmith gestured up the track. He was broad as he was high and most of him was covered in a vast leather apron. 'You'd best be on your way,' he said, 'you've been sent for.'

Jenet Gwen was approaching down the track and Patience was glad of her supporting arm to help her up the hill. With a wave in the direction of the forge, the two girls began the climb. The track was narrow and stony, but Patience barely noticed it. She was still feeling the rush of air past her face and Hywel's strong arm around her waist. How old could he be? He had the face of a boy, but the strength and confidence of a man. She wanted to ask Jenet Gwen about him, but felt sure she wouldn't understand her reply – she communicated in a series of rapid gestures and muted sounds which Motreb could interpret readily, but which Patience had yet to learn.

Jenet put her arm around Patience's shoulder for the final ascent and Patience caught the faint aroma of frying bacon on the evening breeze.

12

The Sermon

The farmyard was unnaturally tidy. The cobbles had been swept and the broom and rakes were stacked against the wall. Everything was bathed in the sanctity of Sunday afternoon. Even the hens seemed to be clucking in subdued voices. The kitchen was tidier still, and Xanthe and Patience, perched on stools in their best dresses, tidiest of all. A lace cloth covered the table, the best china covered the cloth, and food of every description was piled onto the patterned plates. Uncle Huw's collar, starched and brilliant white, made his neck and face seem more sunburnt than ever, and Motreb's corset creaked as she leaned forward to refill the cups.

At the head of the table the Reverend Elijah Tonks was putting away his second chicken pie and his fourth cup of tea. Now and again he would pull a lawn handkerchief from his breast pocket and dab delicately at his damp, bald head. He had a face like the reflection in the back of a spoon and Patience had disliked him from the moment he arrived. It was not so much that he was greedy and took two of everything, or even that he was vain (he had a tendency to peer at himself in any reflecting surface). What Patience really disliked was his patronising tone of voice and the way he corrected their behaviour – even her aunt's and uncle's. They were to leave for the chapel and the great sermon at twenty to six, but now it was only ten past five – another half-hour of sitting, stiff and still, while the Reverend Tonks listened to the sound of his own voice, and the expressions of all present made it clear that he was the only one doing so. Jenet Gwen was fortunate – she'd been able to escape to do the milking.

Outside the sky was overcast and the air humid. Motreb looked hot and uncomfortable in her best, black-beaded dress. She rose quietly and turned to the open door, murmuring about 'more milk from the dairy.' Patience suspected a bid to escape (a full jug of milk stood on the dresser). The bid failed.

'Aspire, my dear Mrs Penry,' the minister intoned, 'to be a Mary, rather than a Martha. That way lies true salvation!'

'Somebody had to be a Martha,' Patience thought, 'or you wouldn't have had any tea!'

Three months had passed since Motreb first received the letter asking her to accommodate the minister. Patience had seen the cow parsley give way to tall foxgloves and had seen the foxgloves replaced by rose bay willow. Her face and hands had become almost as brown as Xanthe's and she knew she had grown – her best dress was a good inch too short and uncomfortably tight across her chest. Florence had insisted that Patience send her measurements so that she could bring a new dress with her on her promised autumn visit. Patience longed to see her again and had hung a little chart next to her bed so that she could cross off the days. Of Hywel or Diamond she had seen little since her uncle's recovery. She wondered if Hywel would be at the chapel.

'. . . miserable sinners that we are . . . answer the call . . .' Perhaps the minister's words were drifting up the chimney with the smoke and helping to form the dismal, grey pall of cloud that lay over the hills. Huw ran a finger around the inside of his collar.

It had been the hottest, driest summer any of them could remember and Patience had often gone barefoot. An evening ritual, after milking, was for her to race with Jenet Gwen all the way down to the stream at the valley bottom to paddle amongst the cool rocks and splash each other with water.

Xanthe preferred more ladylike pursuits. She had made the dairy her special domain, turning out neat little cheeses and pots of butter and arranging them around the inside rim of the well to keep cool until market day. Patience no longer begrudged her the role: turning the handle of the butter churn and squeezing the cheese dry was tedious work and you had to be continually washing your hands. Feeding the calves and prodding the piglets was much more fun. It sometimes seemed to Patience that Xanthe had joined the ranks of the grown-ups and that

Jenet Gwen, although at least a year older, had rediscovered her childhood.

The grandfather clock struck two clear notes. Half past five. Patience gazed at the wart on the Reverend Tonks's chin. She wondered how many of his unwilling listeners had actually succumbed to a fatal attack of boredom and died.

At last, chairs were scraped back, the minister requested a parting glass of brandy 'to preserve his voice for the Lord' and Motreb Ann went in search of the best bonnets. Elijah swallowed the brandy in one, rose, and to Xanthe's surprise, took both her hands in his. Looking soulfully up at the side of bacon, swinging from the rafters, he declared, dramatically. 'And I fervently believe that the Lord has led me to your dwelling that I might acquaint the congregation of the ways the devil has wrought his evil and of how the Almighty has preserved you!' His eyes popped open. 'Will you have the goodness to sit beside the pulpit this evening?'

Xanthe was taken aback. She looked questioningly at Huw.

'I see no harm in it,' Huw said slowly, 'if that is what you wish. Provided, of course, that Xanthe does not object.'

Xanthe looked uncomfortable. She was clearly not happy with the idea but reluctant to refuse.

'Very well,' she replied, resignedly.

'Thank you, my childl' the minister beamed. 'Great shall be your reward in Heaven!'

Out in the yard Gwilym had harnessed Dolly to the wagon and was standing holding her head. It was a versatile conveyance. The front seat ran the width of the vehicle. It was upholstered in leather with a wooden back. Huw climbed in and took the reins, the Reverend Tonks beside him and Motreb Ann at the end. Behind them the three girls seated themselves on a wide, wooden plank, removable when the wagon was needed to transport hay or livestock. Gwilym fastened the tailgate.

'Three black crows flew over the house as you came out!' he intoned in his guttural voice. 'There's trouble ahead – you can be sure of it!'

Patience laughed. Gwilym was never happier than when predicting disaster. As they drove out of the yard, she gave him a cheery wave and he gazed dolorously after them, shaking his head.

It was a relief to be out of doors after the prolonged sermon in the kitchen. Another sermon lay ahead, but at least they would be in different surroundings with other people to look at. The air felt thick and oppressive as they drove downhill between gorse and heather and the sky had taken on an ominous, purple hue, blending to black where it met the horizon. Motreb's best bonnet bore a tall, black feather shaped like a question mark. It stood erect above her round head, fluttering and looking as if she were questioning the whole enterprise.

The girls had attended chapel every Sunday since their arrival. It was a large one, built when the slate mine had been flourishing, to accommodate the workers and their families. Patience imagined how it would have been years ago, when the minister had been her mother's father. She had often pictured the little girl her mother had once been, sitting dutifully in the family pew and, later, attracting the dark-eyed glances of the young John Penry. Now the local community seldom occupied more than the first six pews and the minister was shared with another chapel over the hill. But as they reached the main road and turned left past the forge, it became clear that today was different.

The road was lined with people in their best clothes. Some had evidently come a long way and several of the older women wore traditional stovepipe hats and chequered shawls. They pressed themselves against the hedgerow as the carriages and wagons converged. By the time the chapel came in sight, Dolly was brought to a standstill in the crush.

Patience's latent unease grew. Would Xanthe have agreed to the minister's request if she had known how many people would be present? The clamour of voices and wheels increased, and when it became known that their wagon contained the Reverend Tonks himself, the crowd parted and vehicles were drawn aside. They advanced up the chapel driveway and pulled up before the doors. Patience glanced concernedly at Xanthe's tense face. The whole purpose of bringing her to the seclusion of Hafod would surely be defeated if her situation was about to be broadcast to so many. The crowd flowed between them. It was already too late. Thunder rolled distantly over the mountain and a few large raindrops splattered the flagstones. Usually they sat in the front, below the pulpit, but the pews were filling so rapidly that Motreb Ann led Jenet and Patience up the stairs to the gallery that ran right around the top of the building in the shape of a U. They made their way to the far end, sitting down immediately above the pulpit, facing the entrance. Still more people flowed through the door as the crunch and clatter of wheels continued outside.

Patience leaned forward. Below her, Elijah Tonks's pink head glowed damply, the top of Xanthe's green bonnet very still beside him. Uncle Huw appeared in the gallery, stepping over feet and apologising before taking his seat next to Jenet Gwen.

Peppermint, camphor and perspiration formed a pungent aroma all around. The chapel was now full to overflowing and the doors were left open for the many who remained outside to hear what they could. Patience caught a brief glimpse of Hywel sitting below next to his mother. He looked stiff and uncomfortable in a worsted suit.

'Where have they all come from?' she whispered to her aunt, 'and who are they all?'

'All sorts,' Motreb answered in a hushed voice. 'Farmers and cottagers from around here, and a lot from further afield. There are a few of the *crachach*

– the nobs – in the front pews.' She indicated two ladies fanning themselves and a gentleman carefully placing a silk hat on the floor at his feet.

The muted voices began to fall silent and the minister introduced the visiting preacher. Majestically, Elijah Tonks rose to his feet. All eyes were fixed on his face. He seemed to have acquired a certain dignity and when he spoke his voice rang out with a new resonance and force.

'Dear friends in the Lord,' he began, 'the text for my sermon this evening is taken from the Book of Exodus, chapter twenty-one, verse sixteen.' He paused and, raising his right hand aloft, began in ringing tones to recite his text.

'He that stealeth a man and selleth him, or if he be found in his hand, he shall surely be put to death!'

He lowered his hand slowly and looked around with studied timing at the attendant congregation. Supper table bore that he was, it was evident that, once in the pulpit, Elijah Tonks was an actor to his fingertips, and Patience began to understand the reason for his popularity.

'What,' he continued quietly, 'do we in Denbighshire know of the evil practices of buying and selling our fellow human beings? How can we, far as we are from the lands where these foul deeds take place, be concerned about them? And why do I choose to confront you in the mountain fastnesses of Wales, my brethren, with the plight of those who labour in chains to bring profit to their masters?' His voice had gradually risen to a crescendo, but again it dropped almost to a whisper.

'Because you see before you a young and innocent girl!' – he paused and extended an arm to where Xanthe sat – 'who, like the Israelites before her, was the victim of the cruel and vicious system of slavery, who has sought refuge here amongst us, and for whose deliverance it behoves us all to fall on our knees and give thanks!'

His arm fell to his side and he bowed his head with closed eyes. Every eye in the building was on Xanthe and Patience's heart went out to her. She sat motionless, head bent, and Patience knew that she must be longing to drop through the floorboards out of sight. Uncle Huw frowned in concern and Patience felt her face redden with anger. Elijah Tonks had shown not the smallest interest in Xanthe until it was time to leave for the chapel. He had clearly seen her purely as an embellishment to his sermon – his concern for her was entirely bogus.

Only when he began to enlarge on his theme and assert that they were all slaves to their baser natures, was Patience able to relax a little. Xanthe was not referred to directly after that, but the sermon seemed interminable. Outside the peals of thunder grew louder and sometimes the minister had to raise his voice to be heard above them.

At last he announced the closing hymn. The relief was enormous. The congregation rose to its feet and Patience held her hymn-book before her and sang out thankfully. Soon they'd all be out of their uncomfortable clothes and she'd be able to play with Fan. Now that she was standing, the balcony rail no longer obscured her view of the back of the chapel and for the first time she had an uninterrupted view of the congregation below. Her eyes wandered towards the people who were standing before the open door. Suddenly, she stopped singing, her jaw dropped and the hymn-book almost fell out of her hand. She blinked in disbelief, but there could be no doubt about it – there he was! The stranger she had been convinced was pursuing them and whom she had almost entirely forgotten about during the long, summer weeks was standing, hat in hand, staring at Xanthe as fixedly as he had done at the inn yard at Liverpool all that time ago! His shock of blond hair was tangled and unkempt, his face thinner and his beard longer. Only his expression of fierce concentration remained unchanged.

It took Patience a moment or two to take in the meaning of what she saw, but when she did so, her mouth went dry. It couldn't be coincidence that he was there! He had been following Xanthe! And now, at last, he had found her. Remorse overwhelmed Patience. Why had she been so careless of Xanthe's safety? Why hadn't she told Uncle Huw about this man? How *could* she have allowed herself to forget? Xanthe's eyes were on her hymn-book – she was entirely unaware of the man's gaze. Patience turned to her aunt and tried to speak, but Motreb held up a gloved finger. Uncle Huw was out of earshot, the other side of Jenet Gwen. Slowly and chillingly, Patience became aware that she, alone on the face of the earth, knew that her friend was in danger. She measured with her eye the distance between Xanthe and the stranger. There were two verses of the hymn to go before the final blessing. She had to find a way of getting to Xanthe before he did!

The balcony was full and she knew the stairway would become congested the minute that people rose to leave. For a wild moment she contemplated leaping over the rail. But the singing had already come to an end and Elijah Tonks was intoning his final blessing. As soon as the 'Amen' was uttered, a torrent of chattering broke out all around. Patience became desperate. She leant over the rail and called to Xanthe with all the strength she could muster, but Xanthe, engaged in conversation with one of the deacons, heard nothing. Patience prayed that she would remain there until she could reach her. Heedless of Motreb's calls, she forced her way through the phalanx of bodies.

'Excuse me!' she gasped, 'please . . . please may I pass?' Battling through a wall of serge jackets and flannel shawls, she gained the head of the stairs, itself solid with people. She swallowed hard. Xanthe would be there! Of course she would! Abandoning all semblance of politeness and deaf to remonstrations, she pushed her way down, using hands, elbows and feet to get through. On the ground floor the congregation was beginning to thin out and Patience sped up the aisle. The Reverend Tonks was enjoying the congratulations of the gentry in the front pew, but of Xanthe there was no sign! Patience's manners deserted her. She grabbed the minister's arm.

'Where is she?' she almost shouted. 'Where is Xanthe?' Her heart began to pound. The minister disengaged his arm and looked at her coldly.

'I have no idea,' he replied, 'unless she is waiting outside.'

Patience turned and ran.

'Dear God,' she prayed aloud, 'let her be there! If you never answer another prayer in my life, answer this one!' As she emerged into the open, a deafening clap of thunder greeted her, followed almost instantly by a torrent of rain and a rush of cold air. In seconds, everyone had scattered, some to take shelter where they could find it, others to calm their startled horses. Patience raced through the downpour.

'Xanthe!' she shouted, 'Xanthe, where are you?' Blinded by panic, her voice rose to a scream. Heedless of her safety, she sped between horses and carriage wheels, calling as she went, her feet slithering on the mud. Once, she thought she glimpsed a green bonnet, but the face inside it belonged to a stranger. A voice sounded behind her and two hands grasped her arms.

'Patience!' Hywel cried, 'What the devil is the matter? Where are you running to?'

131

'Find her – oh find her!' Patience sobbed, hysterically. 'She's been taken away!' Her teeth chattered and her wet hair was plastered to her face.

'Taken? Taken where – who by?' Hywel demanded. Jenet Gwen appeared at her side and took her arm, Motreb following and Huw holding out a large umbrella.

'Patience fach, calm down!' Motreb cried, 'Xanthe can't be far awayl She's probably sheltering from the rain somewhere!'

'You don't understand!' Patience groaned desperately. 'She's been kidnapped! I saw him! I saw him waiting for her!'

'Saw who?' Huw asked, as his niece's shoulders heaved in helpless sobs. Hywel bent over her.

'Patience, listen!' he said commandingly. 'If you don't calm down and tell us what you know, we shan't be able to help!' His words got through. Patience made a mighty effort and her sobs subsided. They were almost alone – the downpour had dispersed the crowd. The last of the carriages had crunched away, and the caretaker was preparing to lock the deserted chapel.

'Have you seen a dark young lady in a green bonnet?' Ann asked him in Welsh, but the old man shook his head. Huw put an arm around Patience's shoulders and led her back up the path. Dolly waited stolidly under the trees, impervious to the storm, her coat glistening with rain. Patience was helped into the wagon. They all huddled around her and

Huw held his enormous, black umbrella over their heads.

'Now, Patience,' he said, 'tell us what you know.'

Haltingly and still shivering, Patience did her best: how she had first noticed the stranger, what he had looked like, what Ieuan at Bryn Glas had told her and how, once safely installed at Hafod, she had all but forgotten about him – until this evening, when he had fixed his gaze again upon Xanthe's face.

'It's more serious than I thought,' Huw said. 'We had better organise a search party without delay. Come with us, Hywel, and we'll call on your father.' He handed the umbrella to Jenet and took the reins.

The rain had practically ceased. As Dolly trotted down the darkening road, Patience saw and heard practically nothing. Cradled in Motreb's arms, she stared blankly ahead, impervious to her aunt's words of reassurance. Xanthe had gone. She had survived a life of slavery, a flight across the ocean and their journey to Hafod only to vanish before her eyes. She might never see her again. And it was all her fault.

13

The Search

For two hours Patience remained paralysed with shock. Slumped in the back of the wagon, a damp bundle of helplessness and despair, the events of the journey home had passed her by. She remembered little of the urgent conferring at the forge, the hurrying figures, the confusion of voices, the flashing lanterns. She dimly recalled Uncle Huw shouting for Gwilym, as they clattered into the farmyard and she knew that, in the warmth of the kitchen, Motreb and Jenet Gwen had removed her sodden clothes. She was aware that she had been put to bed, but couldn't tell whether or not she had slept. Her limbs still glowed from the vigorous rubbing of rough towels and her throat burned from the trickling drops of brandy, inserted with a tin spoon.

As the last of the thunder rumbled away over the hills, she lay in her bed hoping she had been dreaming, but knowing she had not. Slowly, her memory formed a recognisable pattern of events. She knew that search parties had been organised and that Hywel and his father were involved. She could recall hearing Gwilym affirm that no one had passed through the farm, and seeing him set out over the hill with Uncle Huw, carrying lanterns. The house was silent. She wondered what time it was.

'Xanthe, where are you?' she whispered. 'What has become of you? What are you thinking about?' She reached out and touched Xanthe's nightdress, folded neatly on the pillow. She felt in no doubt that Xanthe and the stranger were together, wherever they might be. Yet there had been no sign of a struggle outside the chapel. How had he got her away? Manhandling her onto a horse or into a wagon against her will would have attracted too much attention. They couldn't be far away! But where? Patience sighed in frustration. She recalled their bedtime conversation the night before: how they had laughed helplessly as they glimpsed the Reverend Tonks returning from the privy in his nightshirt, and how they had gone on to talk half the night away. Xanthe had confessed her fear of cows and Patience in turn had confided her dread of the autumn pig slaughter and of where, when it happened, she intended to . . . She caught her breath and jerked herself upright, as if shot. Of course, of *course* – the perfect hiding place! Why had she not thought of it before?

The dead weight of helplessness was gone. Leaping out of bed, she laced on her boots, breathing rapidly. No time to rummage in the trunk for clothes and no hope of finding any in the dark. She took a blanket from the bed, folded it in half, and wrapped it around herself like a cloak. Silently, she raised the latch and tiptoed onto the landing. Any suggestion of her leaving the house would be forbidden by Motreb out of hand. She peered over the bannister. In the flickering firelight, the seated figure of her aunt waited up for Huw's return. Her chin rested on her chest and her shoulders rose and fell rhythmically. She was deeply asleep.

Patience descended the stairs as if they were made of eggshells, placing each foot against the extreme edge of the steps to minimise the chances of them creaking. Once, Motreb snorted and jerked her head and Patience froze. But the steady breathing resumed and she was able to cross the flagged floor swiftly. The face of the grandfather clock showed half past eleven. The heavy door was unlocked and she had only to turn the knob, inching it around. As she slipped out, a pale form pressed against her leg. Fan had been watching her progress intently and was coming with her. Patience grasped the outside knob of the door before letting go of the inner one and released it slowly.

They sped across the yard. Thunder and rain had given way to wind and the blanket flapped like a sail. Patience felt a pang of guilt at deceiving her aunt and prayed that she would not enter her bedroom until morning. The gate leading out of the yard in the direction of the slate mine was ajar, yet it was seldom used. So much for Gwilym's assertion that no one had passed through the yard! Could she, perhaps, be on the right track? Now and again the wind blew the clouds clear of the moon's face, making the surface of the road visible. Patience peered at the ground for signs of footprints, but the rain had been so heavy that a film of standing water covered everything. Fan's paws made gentle splashing sounds and Patience hoisted the enveloping blanket clear of her boots as they advanced up the roadway. She had never been out at night, alone, before. She made a determined effort not to look behind her. To the left the ground fell away through bracken and scrub. Between the violent gusts of wind she could hear the rush of the stream far below, swollen to a torrent by the storm. She hadn't come this way since the day she and Xanthe arrived. She paused at the point where the road was joined by the steep path they had climbed with Hywel and wondered for a moment whether Xanthe might have been taken down that way and over the stream to the droveway. But the roar of the water suggested that the stepping stones were well submerged and that crossing the stream tonight would be impossible.

From that point on it was new territory. The road wound around the foot of a tall cliff and the muddy ground gave way to rock, with rusty tram rails protruding from its surface. The bare outline of the slate escarpment stood out ahead in the moonlight.

Since leaving her bedroom, Patience had felt only relief that her anxiety could be translated into action. But as she approached the entrance to the mine and the dead crack of slate echoed beneath her boots, her throat tightened and she felt for Fan's head at her side. Only now did she begin to question her impulsive dash out of Hafod. What was she going to do? What did she expect to find? She forced herself to think. If the stranger had brought Xanthe here and was hiding her somewhere in this slate labyrinth, how could she tell where they were? More to the point, what could she do if she found them? What if there were others? Perhaps she, too, would be captured! But, frightened as she was, she knew that anything – even capture – would be better than the helpless misery of the past hours. If Xanthe really was here, and if Patience could find her, at least they would be together, whatever the circumstances.

A high tunnel stretched ahead, the first few yards illuminated by the moon. Patience skirted an upturned truck, its corroded wheels spinning and squeaking eerily in the wind. Then, swallowing hard, she grasped the fur on the scruff of Fan's neck and tiptoed into the darkness. It was impossible to proceed silently. With every step, shards of slate snapped underfoot The wind howled through gullies in the rock and an ancient chain swung and clanked manically from a gantry high above. But to Patience the loudest sound was the pounding of her heart. Only by pinning her thoughts on Xanthe and shutting out images of ghosts and dead shepherds could she find the courage to go forward. Slowly she felt her way along, her right hand following the wet surface of the rock face. Every few feet she stopped to listen for any new noise, but heard only the wind behind her and, ahead, the hollow echo of dripping water, falling from a great height. Her eyes, in the blackness, were like saucers and her stomach felt like a knot of steel. More than once her courage evaporated and she almost turned back. Gradually she became aware that something different lay ahead. She extended both arms and her hands touched solid rock. She felt across its surface. It reached, in great, jagged lumps, from one side of the tunnel to the other. There could be no way through and there could be no choice but to turn back.

As she and Fan made their way rapidly back to the entrance, Patience was forced to admit that her overwhelming feeling was one of relief. Out in the open the moon, almost full, shone out of a clear sky and she could smell the wet earth. She leant against the side of the cliff and breathed deeply. But almost immediately relief gave way to the sickening realisation that she had failed. She was no nearer to finding Xanthe than she had been when she left the farm.

Her eyes wandered across a landscape made desolate by heaps of slag and waste. The roadway had narrowed here to a thin track and some distance below it the moon shone full on a row of derelict cottages, standing as blank and empty as a line of skulls. It was impossible to believe that any life had ever issued from those gaping doorways.

Wearily, Patience called to Fan and turned to follow the track home. If her aunt had discovered her absence, she would be distraught and there would be nothing whatsoever to justify it. Suddenly, she stopped walking and stood motionless. The faintest of sounds had been carried towards her. She waited, straining her ears to the utmost. It came again – a low murmur, almost indistinguishable from the breeze. Then the breeze dropped. This time there could be no doubt. She had heard voices. And they were coming from the direction of the empty cottages.

Patience ran after Fan and tapped her on the rump to indicate a change of plan. Quietly, they retraced their steps. The air was still now and the sound of voices unmistakable.

As Patience stood and surveyed the ruined terrace, it seemed that the only course of action open to her was going to be the most daunting of all. The line of buildings stood less than fifty yards away, a moonlit island in a sea of broken slate. There was no vestige of tree or bush to provide cover and no possibility of approaching stealthily. Patience knew that the longer she prevaricated, the faster her courage would ebb away. She bent to pick up a long sliver of slate and gripped it tightly in her right hand, feeling with the other for Fan's head. Her voice trembled as she called across to the empty windows:

'Who is in there? Who are you?' In the few seconds' silence that followed, Patience thought she would die of fear. Then, unbelievably, from the first cottage a voice – Xanthe's voice – called back: 'It's me, Patience! I'm in here!'

Patience hurtled down the slope, her feet slipping on the breaking shards. Arms outstretched, she flung herself across the empty doorway of the first cottage, her chest heaving. She had no idea what she was expecting to find apart from knowing that, whatever it was, it was bound to be dreadful.

Nothing could have prepared her for the scene she came upon as she gazed, open-mouthed, into that roofless hole, where every detail was illuminated by the white light of the moon. There, seated on a pile of stones, was Xanthe. She was bareheaded, her bonnet strings around her neck and her hands folded in her lap. She looked as serene and composed as if she had just been invited to tea. Opposite her, his back to the wall, the tense, wary figure of the stranger stared back at Patience. His hands, hanging at his sides, were tightly clenched. Fan lowered her head and growled. Keeping her eyes fixed on the man's face, the little dog skirted the derelict room until she was crouching between him and Xanthe. He took a step back. Xanthe rose and approached Patience.

'Patience, I'm sorry . . .' She held out both hands. 'I know I must have caused anxiety. But I'm quite all right – quite safe. This is my friend. He's been looking for me for months. He's in deep trouble and I'm the only one that can help him!'

Patience stood motionless in the doorway, looking from one to the other and breathing heavily. Disconcerted by her silence, Xanthe's voice became anxious. 'I left a message – you did get it, didn't you? But I've been longer than I intended and . . .' Her words trailed into silence and she moved back as Patience advanced, rigidly, towards her. Something had snapped inside Patience. All the anxiety, misery and fear of the past five, endless hours had become precipitated into a core of cold rage.

'You!' she whispered, 'you . . .' Her voice rose. 'Sitting out here talking! Talking to your *friend*! Do you know what you've done to us all?' She seized Xanthe by the shoulders and shook her mercilessly. 'Do you know what you've done to *me*?'

Xanthe closed her eyes and Patience gasped as two hands forced her hands away. She heard the stranger's voice behind her.

'If you want to 'ave a go at anyone, young lady, you'd best choose me. This is all my doing – Miss Xanthe ain't done no 'arm to no one!'

Seeing the man take hold of Patience, Fan growled, ready to spring. Patience dropped her arms weakly to her sides and motioned Fan away. Then, collapsing onto the stony floor, she covered her face and sobbed. Xanthe knelt beside her.

'I'm so sorry! I didn't know what to do – what else could I have done? When you understand . . .' She placed an arm around Patience and waited for the sobs to subside. Patience leant against her.

'Will you come home now?' she asked tremulously.

Xanthe nodded. Gently, she wiped her friend's wet face.

'I know I've upset you dreadfully and I'm truly sorry, but – there's something I must explain before we go back – before we meet the others.'

Patience, exhausted, waited for Xanthe to go on.

'Do you remember,' Xanthe asked, 'that I told you how, when Mother and I were on board ship, we were kept alive by a sailor who left us part of his rations every day?' Patience nodded. 'Well, this is that sailor. His name is Gabriel Fletcher. He's been searching for me because he's wanted for the murder of Captain Manders and I'm the only person alive who knows he didn't do it!'

Patience looked blank. Battered by stress and exhaustion, her brain felt like putty. She struggled to adjust the beliefs she had held for so long about the man who stood before her.

'So you don't want to harm her?' she asked him.

He smiled wryly and shook his head.

'Last thing in the world I'd want to do!' He spoke slowly in an accent Patience didn't recognise. 'Besides which,' – he approached cautiously, his eyes on Patience's face, and sat down beside them – 'I need her. If she don't testify for me, I'm for the gallows without a doubt!'

Patience gasped. She looked at Xanthe.

'The reason I've been away so long,' Xanthe explained, 'is that, once he'd found me, Gabriel was

143

afraid to remain out of hiding – there's a price on his head, you see. I've been trying to convince him that it's safe for him to return with me to Hafod – that Mr Penry isn't going to hand him over to be tried, once he knows his story.'

Patience frowned. The idea that this young man might need help had never crossed her mind – she'd been convinced for so long that he meant harm to Xanthe. Now that she could see him for the first time at close quarters, she had to admit that he didn't look particularly evil. He seemed younger than she thought. His features, sunburnt and even, were gaunt, and he'd clearly benefit from a good wash.

'Where have you been all this time?' she asked him.

'All over,' he gestured around with his hand, and Patience saw that a grubby bandage was knotted around his wrist. 'Getting jobs here and there. But for the last spell – since I found out where Miss Xanthe was living – I've had to trust to my wits to get by, and lie low.' He nodded towards a makeshift bed of bracken below the broken half roof. Rubbing the back of his hand across his beard, he looked guiltily at Patience. ''Fraid I've even stole some of your aunt's cheese out the dairy some nights, I were that famished. But I'll make up for it!' he added quickly. 'Soon as I ever can!'

'You've actually been to the farm!' Patience was astonished. Xanthe, too, looked surprised.

'So that's where some of the cheeses had got to – I thought I might have counted wrong and I didn't

144

say anything because I thought it might be Gwilym and I didn't want to get him into trouble.'

Patience was looking puzzled. 'If you knew where Xanthe was,' she said to Gabriel, 'why didn't you speak to her before this?'

'Cos I couldn't clean get 'er on 'er own – not without being spotted. Then I 'eard about this big get-together at the church and I reckoned that maybe there'd be safety in numbers. I'd not stand out so much in a crowd, see, and folk as might be on the lookout for me wouldn't think to find me there.' He bent down and pulled off one of his boots, drawing out a dog-eared fragment of newspaper from under the sole. He unfolded it carefully and handed it to Patience, who held it out to catch the light of the full moon as Xanthe leant over her shoulder.

'Wanted for questioning,' Patience read out slowly, 'in connection with the murder of Captain Grayson Manders of the trading vessel *Pride of the Indies*: Able Seaman Gabriel Fletcher. Age: twenty-six years. Height: five foot eleven inches. Distinguishing marks: one tooth missing from lower front jaw; crossed flags tattooed on left wrist.' Patience glanced at the bandage. '£50 offered for information leading to the suspect's apprehension.' She handed the paper back to him.

'Oh Gabriel – you *are* in very serious trouble! But why you?'

'There's a very good reason why me,' he answered. 'An' that's a story on its own as well!'

Patience looked at Xanthe. 'Then maybe we should all go back now and hear the rest at home – I know they're looking for us.' She turned to the sailor. 'Uncle will believe you, I'm sure, if Xanthe explains everything. He wouldn't want the ransom – he's not that kind of person. He knows how you helped Xanthe and her mother on the ship, so he'll be bound to know that you didn't – that you're not a murderer.' She stood up. 'Will you come back with us, Gabriel?'

The young man was silent for a moment.

'Reckon I'll 'ave to,' he said at last. 'I can't stay a fugitive no longer – it's no life. And maybe – maybe I could get some help to prove my case.'

Xanthe smiled in relief.

The three passed out of the gaping doorway, Gabriel ducking low under the lintel. Fan, assured that the stranger posed no threat, ran ahead. The moon cast long shadows before them as they rejoined the roadway, Patience cutting a strange figure in her muddy blanket, nightgown and boots.

'We must hurry!' she said. 'There are search parties out and they're very worried.'

'Search parties?' Xanthe sounded horrified. 'But didn't you get my message?' Patience shook her head.

'You just vanished.'

'Oh!' Xanthe cried, 'no wonder you were angry!' She pressed two hands to her cheeks as they hastened in the direction of Hafod.

'Who did you leave the message with?' Patience

asked her, struggling to keep up with Gabriel's long strides.

'With a lady that I'd seen talking to your aunt last Sunday,' Xanthe said. 'I asked her to tell the young lady that was with Mrs Penry of Hafod that I'd met an old friend and that I'd join them at the farm later. I never imagined,' she added guiltily, 'that it would be *this* much later! And once Gabriel had told me who he was and why he needed my help so desperately, he was anxious to get away from the crowds as quickly as possible, you see. I can see that it was thoughtless of me, but I just *had* to try to help him!'

'I wonder,' Patience pondered, 'if the lady you gave your message to spoke to Jenet instead of me, not knowing that she couldn't hear? I wasn't with Motreb, you see. I was rushing about the place in a blind panic, looking for you.'

Xanthe looked at her. 'Panic? Why?' Patience bit her lip. She'd been in two minds whether to disclose that she had known for three months that Gabriel was looking for Xanthe. Now that she understood his reasons she felt even more guilty about it. The sky ahead was beginning to lighten a little. They slackened their pace as Patience recounted how she'd first noticed Gabriel in the inn yard, what Ieuan at Bryn Glas had said about him and what she feared his intentions might have been.

'That'll teach me,' she said ruefully, 'to keep things I don't understand to myself!'

'But,' Xanthe put in, 'I wouldn't have known any differently. I had no idea what Gabriel looked like until today. We never saw his face, you see, when we were in the hold. I'd have had the same fears as you!'

'I reckon,' Gabriel said, speaking for the first time since they'd left the ruined cottage, 'that we'm all the victims o' circumstances. We ain't none of us to blame. Convincing others'll be a different story, though!'

Patience nodded, worriedly. The next task was to convince Uncle Huw that Gabriel posed no threat to their safety – that he needed their help.

Voices sounded ahead as they approached the farmyard gate. Suddenly Gwilym and Uncle Huw rounded the bend. Both girls were unprepared for the speed of the events that followed. The moment he saw them, Huw gave a shout and in seconds Gabriel lay pinned to the ground. The protests of Patience and Xanthe changed nothing, nor were they heard, as Gabriel was manhandled to his feet, his arms pinned behind him and his pockets searched. Gwilym disarmed him of a jack-knife and handed it to Huw. Motreb and Jenet Gwen came running from the farmhouse and flung their arms around the two girls. Gabriel submitted to his treatment in silence. Only when it became clear that he had no intention of putting up a fight and when Motreb's sobs of relief had subsided, could they make themselves heard. Huw, grey-faced and grim from four hours of fruitless searching, listened in disbelief to Xanthe's impassioned appeal on Gabriel's behalf.

Daylight was growing and a few hens clucked mournfully around their feet as they stood by the open gate. When Huw addressed Gabriel, his voice was severe.

'These young women believe your story, it's clear,' he said, 'but they've been missing for many hours, and you've been with them. They are my responsibility and I intend taking no risks. As for you,' – he paused – 'I know nothing of you. You will remain in my barn, which I will lock, until we've all had some sleep. Then, in the morning, we will consider what is to be done.'

The group moved in subdued silence into the yard. Patience's shoulders drooped. The reassurance she'd given Gabriel was beginning to sound hollow. She knew Huw had had a shock and was not to be lightly won over. As Gwilym led Gabriel towards the barn, she touched her uncle's arm.

'Uncle Huw,' she said softly. He looked down at her white face, streaked with rain, tears and mud. 'I . . . don't think one of us will sleep a wink until we know that Mr Fletcher will be safe.' She swallowed nervously. 'May he – that is – could we settle things now?' Huw's expression softened a little. He passed a weary hand across his eyes.

'Very well.' He called to Gwilym and jerked his head to indicate that Gabriel was to join them in the house.

'I'm a-willin' to tell you all you want to know, sir,' Gabriel said as they entered the kitchen, 'but . . .' – he glanced uneasily at Gwilym.

'You'd best go down to the forge, Gwilym,' Huw said, 'and let them know the girls are safe. But come straight back and don't leave the yard. I may need you.'

Gwilym nodded, throwing a black glance at Gabriel, as he slouched towards the door.

Patience collapsed onto a settle, Xanthe beside her. Jenet, unwilling to release the arm that gripped Patience tightly around the waist, sat at their feet. Patience stroked her hair gently. What distress they had caused! It was useless looking for scapegoats! Gabriel was right – there were none.

Motreb was sprinkling nutmeg onto a pan of hot milk and ladling it into tankards. She handed them around. As Gabriel took his, Patience noticed how white he looked. The wrists that protruded from his frayed sleeves were incredibly thin and she saw that he was gripping the edge of the table. He looked down at Ann and spoke reticently.

'Could I trouble you for a bite to eat, ma'am – I ain't took no food for three days.' Motreb's mouth turned into an 'O' of dismay. Hurriedly, she prepared a platter of bread and cheese. Huw motioned Gabriel to a chair and the group watched the food disappear more rapidly than any of them would have believed possible.

'It's been a night we could all have done without,' Huw told the newcomer. 'You'd best keep your story short.' Gabriel nodded. But as soon as he began to speak, it became clear that the promise was unlikely to be kept. The grandfather clock ticked quietly in its corner and five pairs of eyes rested on Gabriel's face. His voice was soft and slow.

He'd joined the navy at sixteen, he told them – ten years ago, after his father had died and their farm in Somerset had to be sold, and joined a merchant vessel at Bristol. Sailors could be a rough lot, but at the end of a voyage there'd always be pay to take home and by and large he'd never regretted his decision to go to sea. Not, that was, until he'd joined the *Pride of the Indies*.

'That,' said Gabriel, 'that were a bad move. 'E were a villain, were Captain Manders, and I won't never forget that voyage!' His blue eyes were focussed on the fire, but his listeners could tell that he was seeing a very different scene – far away from the farmhouse kitchen. His body stiffened and he clenched his fists. He was doing more than seeing that scene. He was actually there.

14

Gabriel's Story

Gabriel sat huddled in a corner of the fo'c'sle, listening to the gale, as it beat against the prow of the *Pride of the Indies* and lashed at the rigging. He thanked his stars that they were moored in the Mersey and not tossing on the open sea. Six hours to go before the tide would turn, and another four before they could steer safely to port. The deck beneath him rose and fell, sometimes from the violent motion of the waves and sometimes from the quantity of rum he'd put away that evening.

He was meant to be on watch. But with the ship lying at anchor, the bo'sun lying drunk, and the captain and first mate more or less so, there seemed little point in pursuing his duties too rigorously. He leaned heavily against the bulkhead. The rain clouds were moving away, but the wind blew as vigorously as ever. The stamping and roaring of the crew below decks made the ship's timbers shake. Somehow, the bo'sun had got hold of the key to the grog locker and had left it ajar. Liquor had flowed freely, Gabriel taking his share, and with the end of the voyage so nearly in sight, the officers had abandoned any attempt at imposing discipline. The first mate, in any case, had been shored up with the captain in his cabin ever since they'd dropped anchor and showed no signs of coming out. Gabriel doubted that either of them had a leg between them to come out on. Above the rail, he could make out the harbour lights of Liverpool, pitching and falling. His stomach lurched and he looked away. Thank God they'd be ashore in the morning. He closed his eyes.

It had been a wretched voyage from the start. Even before he'd joined the ship Gabriel had known well enough that Manders was notorious for his dishonesty and his evil temper. Back in the days when it had been legal, he'd done a lucrative trade in slaves and was accustomed to treating his crew, too, like so much cargo.

Gabriel had signed on at Antigua because it was the only sailing vessel bound for England at the time and he'd not seen his mother for eight months. He reckoned that if he kept his head down and used his common sense, he'd be able to keep out of trouble and survive. But when they set sail from St John's, Manders had been able to recruit only a little over half of the men he needed to man the ship properly, and they a rag-bag of drunks and reprobates with little knowledge of seamanship between them. The whip was never out of the bos'un's hand and it was a miracle they managed to stay on course. Gabriel was one of the few practised sailors aboard and the bos'un – and Manders – had the sense to leave him pretty well alone.

But there'd been one incident when Gabriel had not been so lucky and he was still seething over it. He'd brought the pay from his previous voyage aboard, concealed in a sock, and, knowing better than to entrust it to any of the officers, had stowed it beneath his bunk. Two days out of St John's it was missing. He'd gone straight to the captain. Manders had nodded sagely.

'You're a lucky man, Fletcher,' he'd told him in his reedy voice. 'Thanks to the vigilance of my Number One, your money is in safe keeping. You may claim it from me when we dock.' The captain's fishy eyes had stared back at him and Gabriel knew then that his money was as good as lost. But two hours ago, when they'd dropped anchor at the mouth of the Mersey, he'd decided to approach Manders again.

Seated in his cabin, the captain and his first mate were already showing signs of having made inroads into the rum. The sailor put his case for the return of the money.

'Money, Able Seaman, money?' the captain leered. 'I don't remember this, do you, officer?'

'Certainly not, Captain!' replied the first mate. Both men were grinning across at Gabriel from behind the captain's desk and Gabriel fought hard to keep his temper. Then the captain's expression had changed.

'Get to your post, Fletcher!' he barked, 'or you'll be disciplined!'

As Gabriel turned away, their laughter followed him.

Now he opened his eyes. The west wind, blowing directly onto his face, had sobered him up. That money was his! He'd worked for it! He thought of his mother in Bristol, counting the days to his return. If there were any way on earth of claiming his dues, he'd find it! He thought hard. The gale still blew and the timbers creaked loudly. But suddenly, amidst the noise, he caught the sound of an unfamiliar voice below. The voice had been female and he knew instinctively who it must be. He leapt to the rail of the fo'c'sle and peered down through the gloom.

Soon after he'd gone on duty he'd noticed the figures of the dark woman and the girl slipping into the cabin that the late Mr Clark had occupied before he took sick and died. A wise move. Discipline had collapsed and those seamen that could trust their legs were roaming the ship at will. It would only have been a matter of time before one or the other of them would remember the two women from Antigua eking out their existence in the hold. Gabriel had been aware all along of how pathetically vulnerable they were, but knew he dared not risk showing his concern. Each morning he'd caught a glimpse of the face of the young girl as she'd retrieved the water and the biscuits he'd secreted to them. He peered in the direction of the cabin where they'd taken shelter. The voice came again and this time it sounded like a cry for help. He bounded down the stairs.

The gangway was deserted and ahead he could see the cabin door swinging on its hinges. He raced towards it. Inside, a lamp lurched dangerously on the corner of a locker. Gabriel seized it and held it up. A chair lay on its side on the floor, a heavy inkwell beside it – clearly there'd been a struggle. But of the woman and the girl there was no sign. He moved cautiously forward and almost fell headlong over something at his feet. He lowered the lamp and the bloated features of Grayson Manders gazed sightlessly at him from the floor. The face was purplish red and the scant hair lay across the brow in a carefully arranged line of thin, grey curls. There was no room for doubt – the captain was dead. Gabriel was well aware of the danger he was in, alone beside the captain's corpse. But deliberately he placed the lamp back on the locker and glanced, cautiously, out of the door. Still no one near. He knelt and swiftly ran his hands through the dead man's pockets. He could think only of the injustice that had been done to him as he searched for the keys of the captain's safe. There were none. His fingers moved around the waistcoat and met something round and hard. Then voices sounded. Hastily he closed his finger around the object and tugged. There was a slight tearing sound. Springing to his feet, he sped silently out of the cabin and up the stairway, his heart banging. Footsteps began running along the deck below. The sky was lightening from the east and the wind was beginning to drop.

As Gabriel regained his breath, he unclasped his fingers and saw that he was holding a round, gold watch. He buried it in his trouser pocket. As he did so, the wind carried towards him a sound like a soft splash, as if something was being dropped into the sea. A second later it was followed by another. He frowned in puzzlement.

News of the captain's death had a remarkably sobering effect on the entire company. As they gathered on the foredeck, they heard the first mate assert his command and learned that, once docked, they must remain aboard until the harbour master ordered their release.

There followed a long and wearisome day marooned on board with dry land lying tantalizingly only feet below. A curious crowd gathered on the quay and rumour was rife: there'd been a mutiny; the captain had been strung up on the masthead; there'd been a duel and the captain had lost!

It was evening before the harbour master came aboard and took over the captain's cabin. One by one the crew were questioned. As it became clear that there were to be no startling revelations, the crowd drifted away. The crew was told that the ship and its cargo were to be impounded and that they were to be released on quarter pay. They could return for the rest of their money when the inquiry was complete and the cargo disposed of.

Gabriel could feel only relief at being free of that accursed ship. There was no sign of the woman, or of the girl. He hoped that, somehow, they'd been able to slip away.

As always after a spell at sea, the ground felt as though it were coming up to meet him, but he smiled at the sight of the solid buildings, of horses, children, old men and all the things that told him he had returned to normality.

He turned in at an inn and settled himself into a dark corner to enjoy a glass of ale and a pork pie and to consider his situation. The watch was burning a hole in his pocket. He felt not the slightest guilt about it, but he wondered if it would be missed. How was he going to get rid of it and what would it fetch? Should he leave Liverpool straight away and head for home, forfeiting three quarters of his pay? The idea went against the grain. No one, as far as he knew, had been asked to account for the watch, so presumably nobody knew that Manders had carried one. At the same time, he dared not risk trying to sell it here. He drained his glass. It was getting late and the alehouse was filling up. He slapped a coin onto the greasy counter and strode outside. He'd made up his mind. He'd wait for his full quota of pay and try to sell the watch when he got home to Bristol.

Gabriel was no stranger to Liverpool. He made his way to a chandlery he knew of in a quiet corner of the quay to enquire about lodgings.

'Wouldn't I be delighted to help you!' said the chandler, disarmingly, 'but that Mrs Duffy and I have only the one room! But Mrs Bludgeon, I know, will be charmed to oblige!' He gestured to the toothless form occupying the greater part of the shop's floor space.

'Two shillin's a night wivout breakfast!' announced Sal, promptly, eyeing Gabriel. 'Bring yer own soap – there's a pump in the yard.'

'And I,' put in Duffy, 'will be more than happy to provide the soap.'

Gabriel was not overjoyed at the prospect but knew he was too weary to search further. He nodded assent. As he paid Duffy for the soap, his eye lighted on a small, tortoiseshell comb resting on a shelf. Duffy was quick to observe his interest.

'A man with an eye for quality!' he exclaimed, 'and yours for only sixpence, sir!' The sailor pocketed the comb and followed Sal out of the shop.

'Fer yer wife, is it?' she wheezed, leading the way up a narrow alley.

'No,' said Gabriel. 'For my mother.'

'Ah!' said Sal, 'a bachelor gentleman!' They were in a dark courtyard and Sal scaled a rickety outside stair, which rocked as she pulled herself up by the rail. She wrenched open a door which gave into a room no larger than a packing case and appeared to contain a single bed. Gabriel made to enter, but Sal barred the way.

'I'll 'ave the money in advance, if you please, sir.' Gabriel handed her two shillings.

'Jest the one night will it be, then?'

'I'll be letting you know,' Gabriel told her

tersely. Sal eyed him, breathing heavily from the climb.

'My quarters is below.' She nodded to the bottom of the stair. 'You'll find me there.' The stairway shook again as she descended. Gabriel collapsed onto the bed. It was cleaner than he'd expected. He lay on his side, taking care to keep the watch between his body and the bed, for the door had no lock, and within seconds he was asleep.

It wasn't just the one night, nor yet the next two or three. Whatever the complications of the case, *Pride of the Indies* remained impounded. The crew, Gabriel amongst them, gathered each morning at the harbour master's office, only to be told to return the next day.

On the evening of the fifth day, Gabriel sat on his bed and counted his remaining money, depleted by rent and alehouse food.

Cautiously he drew the watch from his pocket. Perhaps he could risk selling it. He hadn't examined it properly before. He pressed the rim and the back flew open. Gabriel's face fell – it was inscribed! Graceful, curling letters read 'George Grayson Manders'. He couldn't sell it if he wanted to! That decided it. He'd call for his pay tomorrow for the last time and then head for home, whether he received it or not.

He kicked out angrily at the wall, sending a shower of loose plaster onto the head of a passing cockroach. He'd wasted six days in this wretched hole for nothing! He wanted to rush out and fling the watch into the harbour, but he pocketed it once more and lay back on the creaking mattress.

As soon as he opened his eyes the next morning he knew that something was different. Sitting up he saw that the door of his tiny room was slightly ajar. He stood up to close it and noticed something else. He felt lighter. His hand flew to his pocket, but even before he thrust it inside, he knew the watch was gone. He must have rolled over in his sleep! It mattered little who the thief had been, although he found it hard to imagine that Sal's vast bulk could have scaled the stair without waking him up. No doubt she had sent a small emissary.

He punched the palm of his hand in frustration. The implications were clear: Manders had died from an unknown cause and he, Gabriel Fletcher, would soon be known to have been in possession of his watch, as well as having a grudge against him. It could only be a matter of time before somebody put two and two together and made six – he must get as far away from Liverpool as he could and as fast as possible. The remainder of his money, thank God, was still in the other pocket. Enough to buy a coach ticket out of the town.

Quietly, he made his way down the stairs. There was no sign of Sal. Gabriel had spent the previous evening studying a billboard with information about coaches to Bristol. There could be no question, now, of going home with this hanging over him. He must get away in the opposite direction and wait for the whole business to blow over. Turning the corner, he climbed away from the quay and headed for the coaching inn.

'And when I got there,' Gabriel told his audience around the farmhouse fire, 'one of the first faces I clapped eyes on were Miss Xanthe's – tho' I didn't know 'er name then, o' course.' Patience recalled the scene in the yard of the Gascoyne Arms, the noise, the smell of horses, straw and leather, the apprehension in the pit of her stomach, and the sight of Gabriel's eyes fixed unwaveringly on Xanthe's face.

'She looked so smart,' Gabriel went on, 'I could scarcely tell it were 'er. But then I 'eard 'er voice and I knew for sure who she were.' He looked across at Huw. 'That were afore any "Wanted" notice come out. I nivver saw that till I picked up an old newspaper weeks later. But I knew it'd only be a matter o' time and that Miss Xanthe'd be my only hope if things got bad. That's why I followed 'er coach out o' Liverpool and why I bin tryin' to find 'er all these months – asking from farm to farm.' He passed a hand over his eyes. 'I don't want to get 'er into no trouble, but I can't stay a vagabond, neither. Miss Xanthe's the only one alive as knows 'ow Manders died. P'raps a word from 'er could save my life.'

The group sat in silence, absorbing Gabriel's words. Xanthe leaned forward and looked from Huw to Ann.

'Gabriel kept Mother and me alive on the ship,' she said, 'even though he risked a flogging for it – and perhaps worse. If he's in danger now, then I'll do all I can to help. It's the least I can do!'

'The power to save sailors from death,' Patience mused, half to herself. What would Mr Tresco think now about the name he'd given the tiny slave baby all those years ago in the library of Rose Lea – 'Xanthe – daughter of Oceanus, protector of seafarers'?

Everyone was looking at Huw, seated in the tall-backed settle, as if waiting for him to pronounce a verdict. The early sun sent reflected light through the low window, making a shadow silhouette of his head against the whitewashed wall. He looked thoughtfully at the sailor.

'I don't think you're a murderer,' he said, 'even although you've stolen another man's goods. That's something you may have to pay a price for, you know, whatever your justification.'

'I know,' Gabriel replied, 'and I bin regrettin' it since five minutes arter I dun it.'

'As for Xanthe standing witness for you,' Huw went on, 'I cannot sanction that myself. She has been placed in my care and we are told there's a good reason for her remaining here. The Reverend Morris is better versed in these matters than I and he will be with us – here at Hafod – in a matter of weeks now, perhaps even days. He will be able to

163

judge our best course – perhaps yours, too. Meanwhile, if you can make yourself useful, you can remain.'

He stood up and raised a finger in caution. 'But remember nobody here has seen that piece of newspaper! I'd throw it on the fire, if I were you.'

Xanthe and Patience smiled at one another in relief. Gabriel had closed his eyes and was resting his head on his hand. Now he, too, stood up.

'I'm very much obliged to you, sir!' he declared, as Huw made for the door. 'And I'm right sorry for the trouble I've brought on you all!'

Huw nodded curtly. 'Trouble or no,' he answered, 'beasts can't wait to be fed, nor cows milked!' He looked pointedly at Jenet Gwen, who jumped to her feet and hurried to the dairy.

'I'm a hard worker, ma'am,' Gabriel said, towering over Motreb Ann, as she bent to poke the fire. 'I'll repay you for your trouble any way I can – you can depend on it!' Ann straightened up and nodded wearily. She pointed with the poker to the stairs.

'You two girls – to bed this minute!' Patience saw that there were shadows under her eyes. The strain of the past hours was beginning to show. She crossed to her aunt and kissed her on the cheek.

'This minute!' Motreb repeated.

But sleep didn't come readily, exhausted as they were. It was strange and unreal to be lying side by side in bed in broad daylight with all the activity of the farm going on below.

164

'What will you do,' Patience asked, staring up at the roof, 'if Mr Morris agrees to your going back to Liverpool as a witness? Will you come back here afterwards – or what?' Xanthe shook her head.

'I don't know. Perhaps things will be different by then. Perhaps there will be news.'

'News? You mean about the Abolition Bill?' Patience knew it was never far from Xanthe's thoughts and that, sooner or later, as Mr Morris had told her, Xanthe would be as free as she was.

There'd be no need to fear kidnap in Liverpool, or anywhere else, for there'd be no reward for her return and no market price on her head. Patience realised clearly, for the first time, that for Xanthe, coming to Hafod had been a means to an end all along and had never carried the meaning that it did for her. She tried to push the idea away, knowing that, when the news came, she'd find it hard to feel glad. She drew her knees up under the rough sheets.

'If he does have news – what then?'

Xanthe propped herself up on an elbow. 'What I hope,' she confided, 'what I've always hoped, is that one day – perhaps even one day soon – I may be able to go back to Antigua. Mr Morris mentioned new schools and the need for teachers. If I could do that . . .!'

Patience smiled weakly. She felt guilty at not being able to respond to her friend's hopes. Xanthe bent over her.

'Don't be sad. You might be able to join me there

one day. In any case, we can stay friends, wherever I am!'

'I know we can. It's not that. It's that – well, you seem to have your life all worked out already, and I – I don't know what I want for myself!' Xanthe flopped back on the pillow.

'Perhaps,' she said, 'that's because you have more choices.'

Patience frowned. Did she have more choices? She'd never thought of herself as having any. The effort of considering the matter was too much. The bedroom walls began to swim and, finally, to fade away.

15

News

Gabriel was as good as his word. The first light of each morning saw him cutting peat into blocks, mixing pig food over an open fire in the yard, or cleaning out the cowshed. Farm work seemed like second nature to him and he blended into the daily routine so smoothly that it felt to Patience as if he'd always been there. It took an effort to remember that he'd arrived only a fortnight ago. Motreb Ann was won over completely by the handsome newcomer who called her 'ma'am' and hurried to carry the water for her. Only Gwilym remained implacably hostile, glowering from beneath his black eyebrows and pointedly speaking Welsh in Gabriel's presence. Gabriel made no effort to win him over, accepting the show of resentment as he accepted everything else, with cheerful tolerance.

Patience, now perched on the wheel of the haywain, swinging her bare legs in the early morning shade, watched the sailor drag hurdles across the yard and stack them against every possible bolthole. Soon the sheep, driven down from the hillside by Gwilym, Huw and Fan, would stream into the yard to be sheared. Neighbouring farmers and their wives had already arrived to help, the voices of the women floating out from the kitchen. Patience was waiting for Xanthe to emerge from the dairy so that they could go down to the stream to retrieve two large cheeses, too big to be kept inside the well, which were cooling amongst the stones of the stream and were destined for shearing supper.

Gabriel gave the base of the last hurdle a final kick to wedge it into place and wiped a sleeve across his eyes. Patience gazed thoughtfully at his broad back. She remembered a startling piece of information that Xanthe had imparted to her the night before. 'Gabriel,' she asked suddenly, 'do you *really* have a wife in every port?'

He turned and looked at her with studied seriousness.

'*Course* I do! How else would a body get a clean set o' clothes 'n' a square meal every time his ship docked?'

Patience pondered. 'Who was your very last wife?'

Gabriel pursed his lips. 'My *very* last one,' he pronounced gravely, 'was Gioconda Lagonda from Seville on the coast o' Spain. Where the coconuts come from,' he added helpfully.

Patience consulted Xanthe as they made their way down the steep path to the stream.

'He's teasing you!' Xanthe laughed. 'Seville isn't on the coast and coconuts don't grow in Spain!'

Patience felt foolish. She scowled crossly at her

feet and cannoned into the back of Xanthe, who had stopped abruptly and was looking intently down into the valley.

'What have you seen?'

'I'm not sure. Something small and black – bobbing along the droveway.'

Patience peered over her friend's shoulder, shading her eyes.

'It's a hat,' she said, 'a round one. It's . . . it's . . .'

'Mr Morris!' they both chorused simultaneously, recognising the rotund form beneath the hat. Waving and calling, they dodged between the gorse bushes.

The minister put down his holdall and looked up, his mouth smiling above his beard. The lenses of his spectacles glinted in the sun.

The flying figures leapt across the stepping stones, and before he had time to utter a word of greeting, the breath was squeezed out of him by two pairs of arms.

'Well . . . well!' he gasped, disengaging himself, 'what a wonderful reception! How healthy you both look! And how much more grown-up!'

Out of breath, Xanthe and Patience laughed with happiness, and with one accord the three sat down on the grass at the edge of the water to regain their breath.

'The coachman set me down at the crossroads,' Mr Morris explained. 'He gave me directions to Hafod, but I think I missed the turning.'

'You've passed the track to the farm,' Patience told him. 'You can come this way, but it's steeper.'

'Then perhaps we are justified in taking a rest before we attempt the climb,' the minister suggested.

Patience felt glad they could have him to themselves a little before he became taken over by her uncle and aunt.

'I can see,' he said, peering over his spectacles and using his hat as a fan, 'that country life agrees with you! How are you both, and Mr and Mrs Penry?'

'All well,' Patience told him. 'We've got – oh – such a lot to tell you! So much has happened, and . . .' She paused. Xanthe was sitting motionless, her eyes fixed on Mr Morris's face. Patience knew that, before they could exchange news, the unanswered question had to be broached. Mr Morris knew it, too. He leaned forward and grasped a hand of each, meeting Xanthe's gaze.

'The news,' he said quietly, 'is good. Mr Wilberforce's bill has been passed. You are to be completely free, now, and so are they all!' He nodded gently. Xanthe covered her mouth with her hand and closed her eyes. Patience struggled to take in the enormity of it. Three quarters of a million people, Mr Morris had said, free for the first time! The numbers were hard to imagine. She looked at her friend's quietly heaving chest and knew that she was thinking of her mother, for whom the news had come too late. She placed a hand on Xanthe's arm.

'What a blessing,' said the minister, 'that we have

had this opportunity to be alone together for a while! We have much to celebrate, but much also to mourn, and we need time for both.'

Above them the branches of the ash trees swayed slightly in a sudden breeze that cooled their faces and carried the sound of the bleating sheep down from Hafod. Xanthe wiped her eyes on a corner of her apron.

'Thank you,' she said, 'for coming all this way to tell me.'

'I would gladly have travelled further to carry such momentous news!' Mr Morris assured her. 'I learnt it myself only two days ago. My host at Bala – Mr Pearce – received *The Times* by coach, and we read the report together. Sadly, it seems Mr Wilberforce passed away just days before the vote was taken.'

'What will happen now?' Patience asked. She knew that she was learning of an historic event; that thousands of people all over the world had been praying for this result, and that she must be glad. Yet all she could think about was that Xanthe might be going away – perhaps for ever. The minister sensed her unease.

'Very little immediately,' he replied. 'The bill will not be enacted until August, but when it is, I know that the plantation owners of Bermuda and Antigua have agreed to free their slaves at once.'

Xanthe was following Mr Morris's every word with close attention.

'So when the slaves are free, who will feed and house them?'

The minister pondered. 'The majority will probably continue to work for their former owners, but for a wage. And they will have to learn to handle money – most of them for the first time in their lives. The unpopular planters, such as your Mr Drummond, will, no doubt, lose their workforce quite quickly – although handsome compensation will have been paid out to all the owners by the British Government. As for what alternative employment there might be . . .' He spread out his hands.

'When we last spoke,' Xanthe said, 'you mentioned the need for schools and teachers.'

'Indeed! Indeed!' The little man nodded vigorously. 'And I have not forgotten your keen interest there. I hope to hear what progress has been made with Sir Joshua Makepeace's Education Trust when I return to Liverpool!'

The sun had risen higher and moved around the valley. By the time it was clear of the tree-tops and was shining full on their faces, Mr Morris was thoroughly acquainted with the Reverend Tonks's visit, the identity of Gabriel Fletcher, and the decision that he – Daniel Morris – was expected to make about the sailor's future.

'It seems,' he declared, as he struggled to his feet and brushed the grass from his trousers, 'that I am to assume the role of Solomon! Well, well! Huw Penry and I must put our heads together over this!' As he bent to pick up his carpetbag, Xanthe pointed to a white sunbonnet moving towards them through the ferns.

'Jenet Gwen – come to look for us!' The girls remembered the cheeses and ran to lift two dripping bundles of muslin from between the stepping stones of the stream.

Halfway across the meadow Jenet paused uncertainly and blushed crimson as the Reverend Morris advanced and shook her by the hand, bowing low. Patience mouthed to her to hurry up to the farm with the news of his arrival. The minister gazed after Jenet as they began the steep climb.

'She dwelt amongst the untrodden ways,' he quoted expansively, mopping his brow.

'Well,' puffed Patience, hoisting one of the cheeses onto her hip and already having to raise her voice above the bleating of the flock in the farmyard, 'not exactly. The ways around Hafod are very well-trodden today – we're shearing, you see.'

Motreb Ann had combed her hair and was in a clean, white apron by the time they reached the yard and had negotiated the throng of bawling sheep and sweating men. Huw, rolling fleece into bundles, straightened up and wiped his hands. Their greetings were all but inaudible above the din.

Patience had never seen shorn sheep before at close quarters.

'They're naked!' she exclaimed, as Gwilym parted

a pair of hurdles to allow three of them to bound up the hill, almost bare-skinned and startlingly white.

The kitchen seemed full of women: women stirring, women slicing, chopping and carrying. Mr Morris was ushered into the parlour and Patience whispered into her aunt's ear. Ann gave a cry of delight and enfolded Xanthe in a pincer hug. Patience heard the word *rhydd* – 'free' – passing around the room and spreading out into the yard. Elijah Tonks's sermon had had a powerful effect and everyone knew what the news meant.

Xanthe's hand soon became a soggy repository of flour and sheep oil, as it was clasped and shaken again and again. Patience stood in the shade of the doorway and watched the smiling faces.

Gabriel, emerging from the barn, was the last to hear the news. Bounding to Xanthe's side, he picked her up, swung her around and, to loud cheers, planted a kiss on her forehead.

'We'll have extra reason to celebrate tonight!' Huw Penry said. Xanthe, embarrassed, made her way to Patience's side.

'Do I look any different?'

'Not that I can see,' Patience laughed. 'Just a bit grubbier!'

Xanthe stuck her tongue out and turned to join the women in the kitchen.

Through the open doorway of the parlour Patience saw that Mr Morris, seated before a tankard of ale, was beckoning to her.

'In all the excitement, Patience, I almost forgot!' He delved into his jacket pocket and produced a crumpled envelope. 'Your mother wrote to me a week ago with some excellent news, although it seemed to trouble her a little. She wanted my advice. Here – read this!' He pulled out the letter and handed it to Patience, pointing with a stubby finger to the second paragraph.

Rapidly Patience scanned the familiar, neat handwriting.

'I have received,' she read aloud, 'a most mysterious letter, unsigned, but in a hand I seem to recognise. It advises me that the sum of one hundred pounds had been deposited in my name with Pendleton and Pendleton, solicitors of Dock Street in Liverpool and that I am to claim it in April of next year (when I may have the option of leaving my service here) – so that I may 'build my house upon a rock!' Patience looked in amazement at the minister's smiling face. She read on: 'I hardly know what to think. It would seem to answer all our prayers, for I could establish my dressmaking business within a year and my dear Patience could join me in it. Yet I fear to trust an unknown donor. What do you advise?'

'What *do* you advise, Mr Morris?' Patience was as bewildered as her mother. The minister chuckled.

'If I were a gambling man, I'd bet a pound to a penny that I will recognise that handwriting when I see it! And when I do – I'll recommend acceptance right away! You know,' he went on, lowering his voice and adopting a confidential tone, 'William Gwyn's devotion to your mother has never waned. But he'd die rather than have her know it. Pride is his middle name. Evidently she hasn't made the connection and I won't burden her with the knowledge – it can be our secret!'

Patience felt stunned. A hundred pounds was the sort of money you read about in fairy tales! But did she really want to be a dressmaker in Liverpool now that she had learnt about tossing hay and skimming cream and feeding baby pigs? She pressed her hands to her stomach in an agony of divided loyalties.

'Patience!' – her uncle entered the little room – 'ask Gabriel to come in here, would you? Xanthe as well – we've some important talking to do with the Reverend!'

Patience nodded.

Xanthe dipped her hands into the pail of water that stood outside the door and shook them dry. Gabriel ducked his head under the lintel and winked at Patience as Huw beckoned them into the parlour and quietly closed the door.

Patience stared blankly at its blacked, oak surface, riddled with knot holes and bumps. She didn't feel excluded, but she knew that, when the door was opened again, decisions would have been made and that life would be different. A small knot of apprehension formed inside her.

16

Shearing Supper

With Huw and Gabriel deep in conversation with the
Reverend Morris, the shearers had to work the
harder if they were to be done by sunset. Only
Gwilym resented it, his dark looks growing blacker
as the afternoon shadows grew longer. Patience
moved methodically from kitchen table to oven and
back, laying the newly baked *teisen* on racks for
Jenet to sprinkle with currants and cinnamon. Now
and again she left the heat of the kitchen to draw
water from the well for scrubbing the baking trays. It
was on these trips that she picked up fragments of
the conversation that floated out of the open parlour
window: '. . . face up to it sooner or later'; 'Sir
Joshua . . . lawyers'; '. . . his best chance'; '. . . the
sooner the better'.

By the time the parlour door opened again, she
had already gleaned what Xanthe later disclosed in
the bedroom: Xanthe and Gabriel were to leave with
the minister for Liverpool the next day.

Sir Joshua Makepeace was to be approached
immediately and asked to recommend a lawyer
sympathetic to the anti-slavery cause to defend

Gabriel. (The question of fees was a problem, but Mr Morris was hopeful that the Abolition Society might help.)

Xanthe was to be available to provide evidence in Gabriel's defence and would stay in the Morris household while the matter of teaching possibilities in Antigua was explored.

As Patience helped Xanthe to collect her clothes together, her mind went back to that morning – a mere eight hours ago – when, perched on the wagon wheel, she had been teased by Gabriel about his supposed wives. It was as if she were thinking about someone else – a little girl without a thought in the world but of paddling in the river. Yet now, the far-away world of politics, the law, work and trade had thrust itself into the little farmhouse and was altering her life.

Xanthe was radiant. 'I can't believe it!' she said, shaking her head. 'To think that I could be back in Antigua – perhaps even by Christmas time – and seeing my friends at Rose Lea!' Suddenly she caught sight of Patience's serious face and sat down on the bed. 'Patience,' she said, 'it's not just that I *want* to go back, although I do, of course. I *have* to go! Do you understand?'

Patience concentrated hard on folding a print dress.

'Of *course*!' she said emphatically, without meeting Xanthe's gaze. 'Of *course* I do!'

The door was flung open and Motreb Ann entered.

'What do you mean by it?' she demanded of Xanthe, with mock severity.

'Mean by what?' For a moment Xanthe looked concerned.

'Coming here to Hafod, getting us all fond of you so that you are like one of the family – and then deserting us! It's not fair, is it, Patience *fach*?' She tucked an arm around her niece's waist and gave her a squeeze. 'But we're having no serious faces here tonight, remember!' She placed a fat finger so close to her niece's nose that Patience was forced to laugh. 'Come on downstairs, the pair of you – we've got a celebration to organise!'

Outside in the yard the last ewe had been released, bleating, onto the hillside and the shearers were completing the end-of-the-day ritual of dowsing each other with buckets of cold water. Then, scrubbed pink, they reclaimed their shirts and sat or lay in the shadow of Hafod's red walls as the women dragged trestle-tables and benches out of the barn and arranged them in a square around the yard.

Supper began with ham and eggs. Patience and Xanthe formed part of a chain, passing platters, oatcakes, cheese, *teisen* and whinberry tart from fireside to trestle-top, Fan doing her best to trip them up. An unaccustomed quiet descended on the yard as the food disappeared. Patience counted twenty-six silently munching heads. Taking her place next to Jenet she saw that Hywel was amongst them and was talking animatedly to a pretty girl with auburn curls whom Patience hadn't seen before. Patience supposed she was the reason Hywel hadn't had time to keep his promise about riding.

The moon, low in the sky, was just visible above the piggery. After three slices of home-cured ham and any amount of pickled walnuts, washed down with Motreb's elderflower wine, Patience began to suspect that she might after all be half-enjoying herself. A piercing squeak coming, not from the piggery, but from Llew Nant-y-Coed's fiddle, announced that he was tuning up and the tables were dragged back to make room for dancing. Mr Morris rose, bowed to Motreb Ann and to loud applause grasped her around what had once been her waist as they set off on a fast and furious jig. Llew's repertoire was limited, but not so his endurance. Patience found that all five of his tunes could be danced to a sort of 'one-two-three-hop'. Sometimes she was partnered by Uncle Huw who favoured a dignified glide and sometimes by the minister, whose style was more flamboyant, but mostly she preferred to jig around on her own, enlivened by the music, the laughter and the wine.

The moon was very full and clear. Only when it was shining right above the farm did Llew drop his right arm and go in search of his flagon. But the yard was not silent for long. Five or six of the shearers formed a circle and, gazing intently into each other's faces, broke into a slow and beautiful song in Welsh, which Patience half remembered her father singing to her as a baby when she couldn't go to sleep. Mr Morris listened with eyes tightly closed, his face upturned and the moon glinting off his spectacles. There was silence for a while before Llew took up his bow again. Hywel grasped his pretty partner's arm and the dancing resumed. But Patience didn't feel inclined to dance any more. Tomorrow morning was creeping closer and she knew that she needed to face up to all the conflicting feelings that she'd been pushing into the background that evening.

Skirting the well, she climbed the bank that rose steeply behind the barn. Soon she was looking down on the chimneys of Hafod. The dancers were moving like small, wound-up toys below her and all around were the newly-shorn sheep, cropping silently and shining white amongst the heather. She had scarcely sat down on the grass before a voice sounded beside her, startling her rigid. Her hands flew to her chest.

'You'm looking like you've lost a tanner and found tuppence, maidy!'

'Gabriel! You frightened me to death! Why are you up here?'

'Tryin' to sort a few things out in my head, like. What's your excuse?'

'I'm trying to do the same. Your things are a lot more serious than my things, though.'

'I wouldn't say that, neither.' Gabriel was chewing on a long piece of grass. He sat down next to Patience. 'If you feel like sharin' 'em I've no objection to listenin' – you've 'ad to listen to me enough, I reckon.'

'I feel guilty talking about it – like I'm terribly spoilt,' Patience said.

Gabriel looked at her steadily.

'It's just that, well, everyone seems so sure about everything – sure about what they want to do, I mean: Xanthe, Mother – even Mr Morris. Not only that, they even seem sure about what they want *me* to do. Xanthe wants me to go to Antigua with her; Mother, I know, will want me with her in Liverpool when she begins dressmaking, Motreb wants me to stay here . . .' She heaved a sigh. 'And I – well, I know that I like being here, but I'm not really sure about anything – not anything!'

Gabriel looked at her quizically.

'Who told you you 'ad to be?'

'Who told me I had to be what?'

'Sure about anything.'

Patience looked blank. Gabriel shook his head.

'Lord knows, I ain't nivver bin sure o' much, and wot I 'av bin sure of 'asn't made that much difference!' He spat a lump of chewed grass into the semi darkness. 'As fer makin' decisions – I reckon when the time comes most folks knows what they wants instinctive, without worryin' at it afore 'and like a ferret wiv a rat. That don't 'elp no'ow.'

Patience looked at Gabriel's bland face. 'I suppose not,' she said slowly. 'And no one *has* told me I have to decide anything – and I don't have to, really, just because everybody else is. At least, not for a while.'

'Course you don't! Long as the sun comes up of a mornin', the days pretty well look arter thesselves in my experience. You'm fourteen, maidy, not forty. Just you leave bein' certain to others for a while!'

Gabriel's voice, relaxed and calm, seemed to lift a huge weight of anxiety from Patience's shoulders. She looked at his handsome profile and smiled.

'Thank you, Gabriel!'

A line of yellow light had appeared above the distant hills. Below them the dancing had stopped and the yard was emptying. Some of the revellers were calling '*Nos da!*' and making off down the valley, singing as they went. Others, out of sight in the barn, were making up beds of hay bales. The neat figure of Jenet Gwen passed back and forth across the beam of light from the kitchen door, collecting up drinking vessels.

'Gabriel,' Patience said, diffidently, 'when you . . . if you . . . when things are back to normal for you . . .'

'When I come out o' prison, you mean,' he said directly. 'If I'm that lucky.'

'What,' Patience continued, 'will you do then? Will you go back to the sea?'

'I bin debatin' that point,' Gabriel said, after a pause. 'An' to tell you the truth, I've got so taken with the life 'ere, I've 'alf a mind to try my 'and at farmin' again.'

'It'd be a lot of work on your own,' Patience said.

'It would,' Gabriel agreed, ''cept that I'm not reckonin' on bein' on me own.'

'But isn't your mother a bit old for the work now?' Gabriel nodded.

Patience looked at him in puzzlement and saw that his gaze had never left the slim figure below.

'Oh,' she cried, 'oh, Gabriel – you've fallen in love with Jenet!'

'I nivver said nothin' like that!' the sailor said, in alarm.

'But you *have*, haven't you?'

'All I means to imply,' he said doggedly, 'is that I knows a good lass when I sees one. And you be sure,' – he jabbed at her arm with his finger – 'that you don't nivver breathe a word o' this, least of all to 'er. I got no notion what'll become o' me yet, see. But . . .'

'But what?'

'If my luck 'olds out – that's to say, if they don't transport me, or worse, then you could do me a favour – if you've a mind.' He drew a small object out of his pocket. 'If all I gets is a prison sentence, then you could give 'er this from me.' He placed a little, tortoiseshell comb in Patience's outstretched hand.

'I promise,' Patience said. Gabriel stood up and Patience buried the comb deep in the pocket of her dress.

'All the same,' she said, as they clambered back down the slope. 'I think she may have an idea that you like her – she's taken a lot more trouble with her appearance since you came!'

The sailor gave a broad smile and leapt down into the yard. Then, seizing a broom from the hands of the unsuspecting Jenet Gwen, he chased her into the house.

17

Departures

Mr Morris's breakfast egg had to be today's. Patience, with Fan beside her, was feeling carefully along under the leaves at the base of the hedge behind the piggery, the early morning sun warm on her back. She knew there was one there – she'd seen the brownest of the hens performing its ridiculous egg-laying song only minutes before. She found it, still warm, under a dock leaf. In the kitchen Motreb was stitching a rent in Gabriel's jacket with stubby fingers.

'They'll never let him off,' she declared, 'if he turns up looking like a vagabond!'

Patience thought that Gabriel looked like anything but a vagabond in a clean white shirt of Huw's with his beard neatly trimmed. As for Xanthe, it was so long since she'd worn stockings and a shawl, they had all forgotten how ladylike she could look.

'Word seems to have got around about our departure,' she told Patience. 'Hywel came to say goodbye when you were collecting the eggs. He has to be at the forge today – his father's taking his sister back to Corwen. She's in service there.'

'Oh!' said Patience, smiling more broadly than she intended, 'was that his sister with him last night?'

Xanthe nodded. 'Are the strings of my bonnet the same length?'

Patience reached up to tie the strings under Xanthe's chin.

'When you are staying with the Morrises,' she observed ruefully, 'you won't notice I'm not there half as much as I'll notice you're not here! What will you think of,' she went on plaintively, 'when you think of me?'

Xanthe's face assumed a soulful look. 'Two cold feet in the middle of the night!' she declared, and darted outside to escape the shower of cold water Patience had scooped up from the bucket by the door.

Mr Morris emerged from the parlour, dabbing at his mouth with a napkin.

'We'll walk down to meet the coach,' he declared. 'No need to get the cart out on such a lovely morning!'

Jenet had gone into the dairy to cry. Patience did her best to coax her out, but she shook her head vigorously, pointing to her blotchy face, which gave Patience a clue as to whom the tears were for.

Motreb squeezed the breath out of Xanthe in a farewell hug as Huw shook Gabriel by the hand.

'I'll do my best to repay you, sir,' Gabriel said, 'soon as ever I'm able!'

'Take Fan with you, Patience *fach*,' Motreb said. 'You'll be coming back on your own.'

Mr Morris was striding ahead with Xanthe as they took to the track. Patience saw that Jenet had joined her aunt and uncle at the gate to wave.

Flies buzzed in the bracken, promising a warm day. At the main road Mr Morris consulted his watch. They stood on the verge and strained their ears for the sound of wheels. Patience flicked some dust from Xanthe's sleeve.

'You've got the letter for Mother?'

Xanthe nodded.

'And you will write?'

Xanthe nodded again. Gabriel had climbed on top of the gate and was balancing on the top bar.

''Ere she comes!' It was the 'slow' coach to Ruthin. The horses clattered to a halt when the coachman saw them. Curious eyes peered from inside the windows. Patience and Xanthe gave each other a long hug.

'We'll be together again – I know it!' Xanthe said, her eyes searching Patience's face. Patience squeezed her friend's gloved hand, not trusting herself to speak. Mr Morris opened the coach door and lowered a little, iron step. He helped Xanthe in. The coachman climbed down to rearrange the baggage and the passengers set about rearranging themselves to make room for the new arrivals.

Patience plucked the minister's sleeve and he lowered his ear to her upturned face. She opened her mouth, shut it, swallowed and tried again.

'Gabriel,' she whispered, 'he won't *hang* – will he?'

Mr Morris turned so that his back was to the coach.

'If there is any justice in heaven,' he replied, 'he will not. His chances are fair. We must pray.'

'Ready for you now, sir!' called the coachman. Mr Morris met Patience's frozen gaze and bent to kiss her on the cheek before climbing inside. Patience knew that she had been given an adult answer, not the automatic reassurance she had been half expecting. She wasn't sure that she welcomed it. And yet there was a kind of relief at not having to worry that she was being humoured.

From his perch behind the driver Gabriel gave Patience an enormous wink. The minister leaned out of the window and as the coach rumbled forward, both men flourished their hats.

'Goodbye!' called Mr Morris.

'Goodbye!' echoed Gabriel.

'Goodbye!' Patience called back. She caught a last glimpse of Xanthe's green bonnet and waved her arms for as long as she could see the men's waving hats. Just before the bend in the road, the horses were urged into a trot and the coach and its passengers were gone.

Patience listened hard until the clop of hooves faded and the only sound came from the branches of the hawthorn hedge rattling in the breeze. She took a deep breath and looked down at Fan, lying quietly at her feet.

'Come on!' she said and, lifting her skirt, climbed back over the gate as the little dog slid under the bottom bar.

Instead of taking the main track, Patience turned and sat down on the grass, her back against the smooth stones of the wall, warm from the sun. She hadn't shed a tear. She wondered why. Certainly not because she wouldn't miss Xanthe. She'd forced herself to get used to the idea of waking to see an empty pillow next to hers and of there being no one to scold her if she entered the dairy in her boots. Xanthe had blown into her life like a wind from the sea, and now she had blown out again. She knew it was going to be hard. But something else was happening. Patience was aware of a strange, new feeling that she couldn't name. She stroked Fan's head absently and gazed at the gnats bobbing above the clumps of rushes. If her life were a book, she mused, it was as if someone had just turned over a page.

She sat for a long time, feeling the warmth of the sun on her face and listening to the 'crunch crunch' of the grazing sheep. Gradually she began to realise that she was taking a new and unexpected pleasure in the sensation of being alone. At last the gnats began to bite and the ground to feel uncomfortably hard. She jumped up, scattering a group of ewes. She decided to take the long way home – across the meadow and up the steep hill behind the farmhouse. Fan raced ahead. The bracken almost met over

Patience's head and for a moment it almost seemed that she could hear Xanthe's voice calling faintly down the hill: 'Payshance!' Startled, she stopped to listen. The call came again, but it was a lapwing, crying to her young as she swooped overhead.

Clear of the bracken, Patience glanced up the hill to the young oak where they'd stopped on the day they first arrived. She shielded her eyes from the sun. Someone *was* sitting there!

'Getting too fat to climb the hill?' called a teasing voice.

'Hywel!' Patience breathed again. 'I thought you were working at the forge today.'

Hywel joined her on the narrow path.

'I was – I just walked over to say goodbye but I missed them.'

'But I thought you'd done that this morning.'

Hywel looked nonplussed. 'Yes – well. You're going to see it funny without her, aren't you?'

'Yes, I am.' They climbed until they reached the grass-grown, upper path. 'Hywel,' Patience panted, 'did you really come all the way over from the forge because you thought I'd be sad?'

Hywel flushed slightly. 'I thought your aunt might be worried about you, and in any case,' – he delved deep into his jacket pocket – 'I wanted you to have this.'

Patience sprang back as he held out something black and wriggling. She looked closer.

'It's a puppy! A puppy for me? For my very

own?' Gingerly she put out a finger and stroked the tiny head. Two black, unfocussed eyes blinked back.

'You can't have her yet,' Hywel said, 'not up at the farm – she's not weaned. You must come down to the forge every day to see her so she learns she's yours.'

'Every day?' She took the little creature into her hands and kissed its nose. It smelt of milk and straw.

'I'll call you Rose,' she said, 'because the rose bay willow's out.'

'And if you're lucky,' Hywel said, 'you can have a riding lesson at the same time!'

'Put her back in your pocket – I'm frightened I'll drop her. Hywel, I don't know what to say. I've never owned a living creature before. Thank you – she's wonderful.' For the first time and just when she didn't want them, Patience was overcome with tears. Hywel took Rose and placed her back in his pocket.

'Come on!' he said. 'Your aunt will be wondering where you've got to!' He set off briskly towards the farmhouse.

Patience paused before following. She drew herself up, wiping the back of her hand across her eyes. Then, adjusting her shawl, and smiling to herself, she stepped out swiftly and lightly across the turf.